DROP-DEAD STYLE

Steve propped Harry in his chair so he wouldn't keel over and hit his head on the coffee table. When he got to the door, he paused with his hand on the knob. Might it not be useful later to know who was sleeping in Harry's bed now?

He went back to the bedroom, opened the door and said "Excuse me..." The lady refused to wake up. So he walked quietly into the room and around to the other side of the bed. The face was partly buried in the pillow. He tried again. "Excuse me." No movement. So he put his hand on the pillow and depressed it to see the face better. The girl's eyes were wide open. But she was not awake. He knew she never would be again. And he knew that he didn't have to worry anymore about not really having a modeling job for Ann Brewer.

MURDER AFTER A FASHION

VERNON HINKLE

This book is for
JILLIAN LIEDER
a
New Yorker

Also,
thanks to
Edward Davidson, Jerry Lacy, John O'Leary,
Janet Sarno, John Sharpe, Phyllis Sharpe
and John Will.

Book Margins, Inc.

A BMI Edition

Published by special arrangement with Dorchester Publishing

If you purchased this book without a cover you should be aware that this book is stolen property. It was reported as "unsold and destroyed" to the publisher and neither the author nor the publisher has received any payment for this "stripped book."

Copyright © 1986 by Vernon Hinkle

All rights reserved. No part of this book may be reproduced or transmitted in any form or by any electronic or mechanical means, including photocopying, recording or by any information storage and retrieval system, without the written permission of the Publisher, except where permitted by law.

Printed in the United States of America.

MURDER
AFTER A FASHION

1

Friday, April 20

It wouldn't have been so bad in the old days before he'd acquired his fear of heights. But now he felt a little queasy being held by the ankles and dangled out his fourteenth-floor, Twenty-third Street office window.

The guy who was holding him (holder) wanted a name, and the guy who was being held (holdee) didn't have it. Not much hope there. Nor could the holdee engage the holder in conversation because the holder was a gesturer when he talked and, under the circumstances, the holdee preferred that the holder kept his hands right where they were. Stalemate.

Holdee: Male, white Caucasian, thirty-five years old. A mere five feet three inches tall, so he's got that much farther to drop. His black hair hangs straight down, but is normally fluffed up to make him look a little taller. He does what he can on top and wears elevator shoes on the bottom.

Just enough lift in the shoes to boost his height, but not enough to remind him every morning he's a shorty. Whenever he is reminded, he consoles himself that Alan Ladd was short.

What he lacks in height he has in muscle. Almost every weekday and occasional Saturdays, he goes to his local YMCA where he runs, takes a fast-paced calisthenics class, lifts weights and, if there's any time left, lets himself sautée in the sauna while he fantasizes about improving his lot.

Up there on the door of his office it says "Stephen Hershey, Private Investigator." When he was in high school, Steve had his career choices narrowed down to detective or pop singer. Because he tended to get lost at the back of the choir, they put him down front with the sopranos. So he leaned more toward detective. He read all the classics in study hall—Mickey Spillane was a favorite—and the dream grew into an obsession that kept hold even after he realized detective work wasn't anything like what he read. There was nothing glamorous about tailing wandering spouses or uncovering financial secrets. Nothing glamorous about the work, but still a stubborn, persistent glamour about the idea of being a private eye. Not at the moment, of course, but at such times when he isn't being held out a window.

Holder: Also male, white Caucasian, early thirties. Even more muscular than Steve and a lot bigger. A hairless ape. He doesn't even have eyebrows. His name is Moe Marshall. On better days, Steve calls him Big Moe.

On better days, these two gentlemen agreed about things. Or at least Steve had the good sense to agree with Big Moe. Having met at the Y, breathing hard and pumping iron, they did in fact share an appreciation for body building. With Moe, weightlifting was a religion.

Next to body building, Moe's favorite topic was women and, to hear him tell it, he was intimate with more than his share. Steve shared Moe's appreciation for members of the opposite sex, all right, but not Moe's attitudes about them. Steve was more liberated than Moe.

One of Moe's uncharming attitudes about women was downright old-fashioned. He thought each of his girls shouldn't be interested in anyone but him. He was used to getting away with it, too. Until about two months ago when one of the ladies in question started to stray.

She was Gloria Emery, a sweet little, blonde-haired innocent who acted like she just got in from some farm in Kansas. She did, but not *just*. It was quite a while ago when she hit town. Moe found her looking lost amidst the cold confusion of the old Port Authority bus terminal and had been her protector ever since. That's what she seemed to need. Until recently. There had been a couple of times when Gloria was out when Moe came to call, and that made Moe suspicious she was seeing another man.

Moe revealed his doubts to Steve one day in the Sally McManus bar where they were celebrating Washington's Birthday. Steve spoke to Moe in his own language. "Dump her," was the sage advice. "She's not the only filly in the stable."

Moe gave that a moment's consideration before he reverted to type. "Like *Hell*!"

"Well, you're probably right. What're you going to do?"

Moe raised his heavily-biceped arms over his head in a Godzilla gesture. "I'm gonna find that bozo she's seeing and pound him headfirst through the sidewalk."

The words of an old song came back to Steve, about a legendary Big Moe who was a digger and who dug in the earth like you dig in your mind. Old songs were always distracting Steve with no regard for the appropriateness of the moment. This one turned off when Steve saw Moe's face light up very, very slowly with—could it be?—an idea?

I just got..." Moe began, then paused in awe. "Yeah, I have. I got me an idea, Steve."

"An idea, Moe? Where'd you find it?"

"Now, look." Moe held out both his hands like he was going to give Steve a concussion by slapping his ears. But the hands paused on each side of Steve's head as Moe indulged in more thinking. His features contorted, and then there was that ghastly light in his face. The hands came down hard on Steve's shoulders, and Steve felt his coccyx touch down on the chair seat. "Now, look," Moe went on in the same vein. "You're a detective, ain't you?"

Steve shifted uncomfortably, partly readjusting his spine, but still feeling like a snake in a mouse maze and wondering how he was going to wriggle out of this. "Sure," he had to admit, "sure, Moe. I guess I am. Once in a while."

"Well, you find out things, don't you?"

"Once in a while, I guess."

Moe gouged the air with his thumbsize finger. "Then you're the guy, old buddy."

"The guy, Big Moe? Me?"

"Yeah. You're a detective, and you find out things. So find out the name of the bozo who's seeing my Gloria. It's a deal!" he decided all by himself and held out his hand. "Put 'er there, old buddy."

"No, no, Moe. That's not necessary."

"Come on, shake!"

"No, that's okay. I trust you."

"Give me five."

Steve gritted his teeth and held out his hand which was met with a grasp that got his phalanges acquainted. Steve hated it when Moe got affectionate, and he hated it double this time. But there it was. The deal was made.

Somewhere in the jungle of Moe's mind, he had acquired such a strong faith in Steve's abilities that he couldn't believe, two months later, Steve still didn't know the name of the guy Moe wanted to use for a jackhammer. The only way Moe could deal with it was to get mad and ornery and decide Steve had to be holding out on him.

When Moe came storming into the office, his neck muscles looked ready to pop blood, his jaws were like great rocks, and he couldn't have looked more threatening if he had eyebrows. "Who's the guy?" he asked, meaning time's up. Not liking or believing the excuses he got back, he jumped up on Steve's desk, one foot on the City Directory, the other landing on a pastrami sandwich. Steve's hand had been on the sandwich, and when he saw that pair of size twelves coming, he jerked back. The force of the move made his faulty swivel chair fall back toward the open window, which in turn sent him out into space. Before he could answer the call of gravity, he felt Moe grab his ankles.

Maybe Moe's first thought was to save his old friend, whether out of concern for the friend's life or the information the friend probably had, who can say? Whatever the motivation was initially, now Moe seemed to find satisfaction in Steve's predicament, and maybe it was a way to get results.

"Make you a deal, okay, Steve?"

Hope supplanted nausea. "Sure. Good idea."

"Just give me the name of the bozo, and I'll haul you back in."

Nausea returned, accompanied by a life rerun that started with Steve's birth in St. Mary's Hospital in Amsterdam, N.Y., and got all the way to the fight he had with that kid in Johnstown. Never could remember his name until now. Harold Fancher.

"Come on," Moe pleaded. "What's his name?"

Immersed in his documentary, Steve said "Harold Fancher." Then he felt himself rising. Once inside, he huddled on the floor and felt like he was falling. It was a while before he felt Moe slapping him on the shoulders.

"Come on, Steve. You're okay."

Since Moe was always right, the words brought Steve back to the third dimension. "Yeah, Moe, like you say. But don't go holding me out any more windows."

"Aw, I was just teasing you. Same way you was me about the name."

"What name?"

"That bozo Harold Fancher."

"Oh! Yeah! Harold Fancher! A tough customer, Moe. I advise you to drop the whole thing."

"Like *Hell*!"

"Well, that's part of my job, advising you. Just doing my job. This guy's *Mafia*, see? He's got a whole army of *torpedoes*. And they'd want to *take you for a ride* and *rub you out*."

"Where is he?"

"Moe, I tell you, he's *Mafia*! He's in the cement shoe business!"

"Where's he live?"

"Am I not getting through to you?"

"Steve, I'm gonna put you out the window again." He lunged.

Steve sidestepped, an instinctive move that turned out to be strategic. Also enlightening. Steve had always placed topheavy importance on Moe's size and strength, and it froze him up. Avoiding Moe's dive and thereby confusing him suggested to Steve that what Moe had in brawn Steve might just make up in agility.

Moe went into a crouch and pivoted slowly like an oversized, lethargic periscope, slowly enough for Steve to hop on his back and complete a full nelson. Moe brought his arms down but couldn't break the hold.

Steve locked his legs tight around Moe's middle, squeezing until Moe grunted.

"Give me a break, will you, Moe? You know you're tougher than I am. Let's call a truce, okay? So I can explain."

"Well, okay..." The words came out pinched. "Okay, Steve, for old times' sake."

Steve dismounted and backed away. "Moe, as a gesture of good faith, how about closing the window?"

Moe did, then sat in the swivel chair to catch his breath.

"Okay, Moe. I've been meaning to give you a full report. Now I don't want to pull any punches, so you've got to promise you won't fly off the handle anymore."

Moe nodded.

"Good," Steve said. "That way I can tell you the truth," and he proceeded to lie through his teeth. "The problem is his being Mafia and being used to being tailed. I think he spotted me. That's why I think we should turn this case over to another detective. A fresh face on the trail might be more effective right now."

Moe shook his head like a slow neck exercise. "You do it. You're my buddy. Want you to do it. Okay?"

Well, of course it was okay.

Steve flinched as Moe walked by him, but the big man proceeded to the door. "See you tomorrow," he threatened, and then the door closed behind him.

Steve sank gingerly into the chair still warm from Moe and grabbed the telephone. He made a desperate call to Rothstein Printing where Gloria worked, posing as a bored kid who was conducting a survey on how people got to work and so forth. Gloria said she'd walked. How far? Not too far. What part of town had she come from? Crosstown, in a way. Which way, east or west? East to west, she thought. Was there someone else living where she'd come from? Her answer was that her boss was beginning to give her the fisheye, and she had to get off the phone. Steve wondered if he could call back at a more convenient time because, if he didn't finish the interview, he wouldn't get paid. Gloria asked him to leave his number and maybe she could call him. Steve gave his office number and said his name was Bobby Harmon.

When the phone rang later, Steve answered it with a noncommital hello.

"Hello? Steve?" It was the girl with whom he was considering living for a while to see how it worked out, and then they'd see.

"Oh, hi, Jody. What's up?"

"You always answer your phone with your tough voice and say, 'Hershey.' Why all of a sudden is it 'hello'?" She always picked up on little things, and Steve hoped he'd never have to try to deceive her about anything.

"Detective stuff, Jody," he tried to explain.

They talked some more, but Steve's mind was elsewhere. He was thinking that Gloria probably wouldn't call back. He was thinking that whenever he waited for Gloria to come home and she did (twice), she came alone in a cab. Whenever he tried to trail her from work and she didn't go home (twice), he lost her somehow. If there was a single conclusion to jump to, it was that Gloria was taking pains to keep her secret life secret. Too bad he'd met her once (in Moe's apartment, about which less said the better) or he could try a more direct approach with her, pretending he was someone else, that kind of direct approach. He decided he'd have to pretend to be someone else with someone else, someone close to Gloria.

His mind came back to Jody on the telephone. He broke the date they'd just made for that evening.

"Detective stuff?" she asked.

"What else?"

"Could be another woman."

Red alert. "I'll tell you Sunday. Okay?"

There was a silence before she said okay back. She said it with a forced brightness that gave him a sinking feeling.

2

In Steve's lexicon, you were either a New Yorker, an out-of-towner or a waffle. This was the subject he'd used to engage Gloria in conversation that time at Moe's. Gloria pigeonholed herself as an incurable out-of-towner because the city scared her a lot. But she had a friend at work, Ann Brewer, who was a waffle, whose feelings about the city—and herself—seemed to depend on how she was feeling from one day to the next.

This was the girl Steve hoped to pick up.

On his way to this objective, as he walked the city streets between his office and Rothstein Printing, Steve congratulated himself on being a dyed-in-the-wool New Yorker. He belongs in the city. He's happy here. Here he can be five foot three and nobody gives a damn.

Gloria appeared outside Rothstein Printing with another girl, and they stopped on the sidewalk to finish some life-or-death conversation.

The girl in question was pretty, short but well-proportioned, maybe twenty-five years old. She stood with her feet apart on a firm base. She had an appealing gnome-like smile and coiffed brown hair. At another time, you might even say she was a beauty. At this time, nobody could compete in the looks department with Kansas Gloria.

The girl seemed to be coaxing Gloria west while Gloria insisted on going east. Eventually, the two girls kissed the air by each other's cheek, waved and went their separate ways.

Steve followed Gloria's friend to one of those would-be pubs. This one was called Jeeve's, an eclectic place that served beer in glass mugs, threw a little sawdust on the floor and catered to a lot of people who didn't smoke.

Steve stationed himself at the bar and ordered a mug of ale. The girl had folded herself into a booth with a boisterous peer group. She didn't seem to belong to any of the three guys near her, but it looked like one of them wished she did. He was freckled (rare in the city) and had sandy hair and was, in Steve's opinion, too young for the object of his affections.

The loud conversation in the booth would periodically come to an abrupt halt, there would be a pause, the girl would puncture the silence with a short comment, and then the others would howl. The freckled kid laughed loudest.

The girl struck Steve as a good-guy type, more successful in friendship than love, maybe a closet dreamer.

Steve checked himself out. He was wearing what he called Motif Number Three, the pinstripe navy-blue vested job with a light-blue shirt and paisley tie. Perfect for Approach Number Ten. Just get rid of the tie and flare the shirt collar out over the jacket, moving from a Straight Three to a Three Casual. Once the tie had been relegated to his inside jacket pocket, he found the appropriate business card in his wallet. It said "Hershey Advertising Agency—Howard Hershey, President" and gave his real office telephone number. Approach Number Ten.

He sent the card to the booth via a waitress. He rationalized that the approach wasn't any cornier than singles bars. And he had to separate the girl from the cohorts with whom she enjoyed being witty and together.

Keeping the card hidden, she squeezed her way out of the booth and brought her purse with her.

Steve met her halfway with his most disarming smile and led her to his vacated barstool. He stood, and she towered over him. One positive thing that could be said about his size was it wasn't threatening to women.

"Okay, Mr. Hershey." She grinned cynically. "What's up?"

"Okay," he said. "You know my name. You are?"

"Agnes Gooch."

"Okay, it doesn't matter what your name is. The point is my company is planning a big promotion for a new skin lotion. In another week or so, we're going to start looking for a model who'll give the product the right image. Have you ever done any modeling?"

"Are you kidding?" Somewhere inside she was frightened. "Well, nothing to speak of, anyway. Just Mickey Mouse stuff."

"In a way, that's to your advantage. We're going to be looking for someone who doesn't look like a model but who still radiates a natural prettiness and sophistication. And you just might be it, if you're interested."

She thoughtfully rubbed at an oval silver plate under the clasp of her purse, then her fingernail traced the design etched there. "What makes you think so?"

"I've been sitting here watching you with your friends, the way they seem to like you, the close way you relate to them. I liked what I saw. It's a good start. But of course there's more to the job than that."

A wary look in her eyes. "What *more* did you have in mind?"

Steve switched to offense. "Look, it'd help if you'd get it out of your head that I'm trying to pick you up. I'm happily married, believe it or not, have two kids and a St. Bernard with arthritis. They all understand me. It'll also help if you understand this isn't a definite job offer. We're going to be seeing a number of people before we make our final decision, but I think if you can relate to the camera the same way I saw you relate to your friends, you've got a good chance."

She was embarrassed now. "I'd be nervous as hell."

"You interested, or are we both wasting our time?"

"I'm Ann Brewer," she said and extended her hand. Steve shook it in a businesslike way.

They were still at Jeeve's when the after-work crowd thinned out. When a booth emptied, they moved into it and continued to drink and talk. Freckleface hung around until it was almost indecent and then, with a brave, melancholy look, he dragged his heels out the stained-glass door.

Ann wanted lots of information, all of which Steve made up on the spot, dispelling each of her fears until he could see her investing hope in this chance to go over the wall at Rothstein Printing. Then the path was open to imagining a glamorous, lifelong career. And that projected to a lifelong friendship with the guy who gave her her first break.

Somewhere, deep down inside where it wouldn't interfere with the job at hand, the guy hated this. This girl was well-adjusted, knew how to cope, when he came into Jeeve's. But her newfound buddy, through accrued guile and booze, had discovered her fantasy and helped her turn it into expectation. By way of getting information he was setting her up for a big fall later. He'd try to find some way to make it up to her, but now there was no turning back from the course that would end, much to Ann's surprise when she thought about it the next morning, with the sharing of confidences.

"Gloria's funny," she told him. "A beautiful girl. Now *there's* someone you'd want modeling for you."

"Oh? Where can I find her?"

"She could have any man she wants, but she gets involved with an ape, some weightlifter type." Now with the lid off, anxieties were surfacing. "It really bothers me. I don't know. She scares easily, so maybe she needed him as a bodyguard. Anyway, that all changed somehow, and she thought she needed a second bodyguard to protect her from the first. It had to be something pretty bad, I mean for Gloria to actually leave the weightlifter."

"How come?"

"She's not the type to take action like that. Something she learned in Kansas, I guess, letting other people take care of her. I guess she was always drifting into protective situations that became intolerable later. Something like that drove her out of Kansas. Something like that made her leave the weightlifter. But this time..." She stopped and stared into her drink. "... She got involved in something."

"What?"

"I can't go into that. Maybe I've gone too far already. Maybe I've had too much to drink."

"Well, is it another protector then? Another guy? Can you tell me that much?"

"Maybe it's another guy, in a funny way. But it's more than that." Her voice took on the sound of desperation. "I'd like to tell you... but Gloria's a very old friend. And she's not the only one involved... and... I think I've said enough."

"Okay."

"This modeling job. Is it on the level?"

"Definitely," Steve lied.

"And could you use Gloria somehow?"

"If you could just give me a telephone number..."

She looked at her wristwatch. "I keep forgetting to buy a battery for this. Do you have the time?"

"About six-thirty. As I was saying..."

"I've got to run. I'm late for an appointment." She gave him a pretty smile. "Thank you, Mr. Hershey. Hope you don't mind me dashing off in the middle of something like this."

"Of course not."

"You wouldn't want to know anymore about Gloria right now. I think... I *know* there's a guy in on it, like you said, but it's more than that."

"If your friend's in trouble, maybe I can help."

"You wouldn't want to get involved, believe me. I mean, the guy might be doing something he shouldn't."

"You mean he's a gangster of some kind?"

"Yes, he might be. He might even be Mafia."

3

Whether or not Gloria had gotten involved with crooks, it was at least clear that something heavy was going on, at least from Ann's point of view. It was also clear that Ann was hiding something for Gloria's sake, maybe for her own, too. Ann might, in fact, be hiding Gloria.

Ann left the booth without her purse, and Steve let her forget it. Once she was gone, he found her address inside it, an apartment building six blocks east of the bar, which was at least in the direction Gloria had gone after work.

The building had a nice lobby with all the obligatory security devices—television cameras in the elevators, a console of screens monitored by a doorman. Doormen could be a problem for Steve who stiffened a little whenever he had to deal with one. But this one turned out to be okay. He volunteered that Miss Brewer had just come in and he rang up to her apartment. He let it ring a long time, then figured she wasn't there after all.

Steve saw Ann on a television screen, on a descending elevator. The purse wouldn't get him into the apartment if he met her in the lobby. So he initiated Plan B, to see if Ann might lead him to somewhere else where Gloria was hiding. He draped a five dollar bill over the television screen and urged the doorman to keep trying with the house phone. The man smiled and buzzed again, obligingly listening to static and not seeing Ann emerge from the elevator and stride out the door. The doorman turned to Steve with an apologetic shrug. "Sorry."

Steve looked exasperated. "Well, she forgot her purse. I was returning it."

"No problem. I'll give it to her."

"Thanks." Steve handed him the purse and the bill.

When Steve got outside, Ann was at the end of the block and headed west. It began to drizzle, and he felt doubly blessed because rain decreased Ann's chances of finding a cab, and trailing by foot was easiest. But a yellow checker came along with obstinate slowness and stopped for her when she hailed it.

This improbable event gave Steve zero odds for getting a cab of his own. But with nothing to lose, he whistled at another cab that was approaching with its off-duty sign lit. Miracle of miracles, the cab stopped.

"Going west, young man?" asked the driver, a delicate Roddy McDowall type.

"Look, yeah, I think so. Look, buddy, my girl and I just had a fight, and I got to make it up to her. She's in that cab. Think you'd be able to follow her?"

"Sure, if she's going west."

Steve hopped in. "We're losing them."

"Say it isn't so." With a wet, rubbery screech, the cab took off, its objective in sight.

Steve automatically reached for a pack of cigarettes as he noted Ann's cab pass Jeeve's. What appointment could be so important that a woman wouldn't stop along the way for her purse? It would make just as much sense to say she wanted Steve to have it.

"Not too close," Steve said. "She'd just get madder if she knew I was following. I only want to know where she's going."

"Not to worry. Not to smoke either."

"Huh?"

"See the sign? We appreciate your not smoking."

Steve put the pack away and felt foolish. This was always happening to him in cabs.

Ann's cab turned downtown. "Oh, oh," Steve's driver said. "That's not west anymore."

"There's ten bucks in it for you if you don't lose them."

"That sounds like it's from a movie. Suppose they turn around and head for Kennedy or LaGuardia?"

"They won't."

"How does one know this?"

"She's afraid of flying. Fifteen bucks, okay?"

"You going to need a receipt?"

"No."

"Then mind if I turn off the meter?"

"No."

When Ann's cab stopped it was the corner of Twenty-fourth and Tenth, an apartment complex called London Terrace that occupied the entire block between Ninth and Tenth Avenues. Ann got out and went into the building.

"Up to twenty if you wait five minutes."

Steve got out without paying and went into the building before the driver could protest.

Another doorman. "Yes sir?" The man's feistiness was barely concealed by his attempt at politeness. He had white hair without being kindly.

Steve acted like the doorman was just another guy and not the bane of anyone's existance. "The lady who just came in here. Miss Brewer?"

"That her name?"

"Yeah. I'm with her, and she went ahead while I paid for the cab. But I forgot the apartment number." He watched one of the two television monitors and got a bird's-eye view of Ann. When she left the screen, the elevator indicator said it was the tenth floor. "I think she said the tenth floor," Steve said. "Can you tell me the apartment number?"

"Not me."

Steve went to the directory displayed over the mailboxes off the lobby, and in his ever-ready notebook jotted down the names listed for the tenth floor. He returned with the list. "You only got ten apartments on the tenth floor in your part of the building?"

"A through J, that's right."

"Then it's got to be one of these." Steve showed his list. "Any idea which?"

The doorman reluctantly eliminated two of the names as being out of town. "Look, you trying to tell me you got no idea where your girlfriend was going?"

Steve pretended to be embarrassed. "Crazy, huh?"

"You said it. I didn't."

Steve tried an offense. "Aren't you supposed to call up and find out if people are home before you let visitors get in the elevator?"

"Sonny, I've been at this business long enough to know who's okay..." He paused to stare at Steve a moment. "...and who's suspicious. I used to be a cop. And the lady was no stranger. If true to form, she'll be back in about five minutes."

"Oh, okay. I'll be right back."

"What if she gets here first?"

Steve went out the door without answering. The rain had let up, but the cab driver was nervous.

"I was on my way home once upon a time," he said. "Why don't you pay me so I can go? My roommate's suspicious enough as it is."

"Roommate?"

"What can I tell you?" The driver gave him a thin smile. "He worries about me a lot."

"Will he feel better if you bring home an extra twenty-five?"

"It'll help buy flowers. Okay, where we going now?"

"Look!" Steve exploded. "I'll be grateful if you try to accept this situation with an open heart and don't pressure me. I've got enough pressure as it is!"

"Easy, easy. What pressure?"

"What are we going to do now? What are we going to do after that? How long's it going to take? How far do we have to go?" Steve took a deep breath and exploded again. "My roommate worries about me, for god's sake!"

"Easy, easy..."

"Okay. I'm okay. But just ease up, okay? Let's try for a workable relationship, okay? I might even throw in a tip."

"Hey, I recognize a situation when I see one. But can you blame me for wanting to know what

I'm getting into? My god, there are a lot of crazy people running around the city."

Steve handed him two fives. "Something on account, just to show you I'm sincere."

"Thanks. What were you saying about a relationship?"

"Just count your money."

The doorman was with Ann when she emerged. He looked around for Steve, shrugged, then went back to his station.

Ann was wearing a fur coat that hung just below her knees and quivered in an odd way as she approached the cab.

Steve crouched low in the back. "She mustn't see me," he whispered.

"Taxi?" Ann asked through the partly open front window.

"Where you going?"

"Kennedy."

"I'm off duty."

She made a scatological mumble through her teeth and walked to the corner to grab a cab that was just being vacated.

"Excuse me, sir," said Steve's driver. "No pressure or anything. But didn't we have an up-front understanding about Kennedy? LaGuardia, okay. But *Kennedy*?"

"Thirty."

The driver followed Ann's cab. "You sure you're really interested in this lady? Wearing a sable this time of year has got to be vanity or insanity."

"She's got a low metabolism."

"Doesn't explain why a sable rides a cab instead of a limo."

They nearly lost their quarry at the Midtown Tunnel where a policeman was shuffling cars through a construction maze, but the driver managed to find the target cab when he emerged from under the East River.

"You know, thirty dollars isn't a great deal if this turns out to be a round trip."

"It's pretty good with the meter off." Steve counted the money in his wallet. Forty-five was his limit in this poker game.

They pulled up at the Eastern Airlines terminal. Steve jumped out as the fur was undulating through the automatic doors. He turned quickly back to the cab.

"Yeah, yeah, I know," the driver said. "You want me to wait, right?"

It wasn't hard following the fur through the crowd, especially one that moved the way this one did, responding to every movement of Ann's body, like it was alive. It moved toward the ticket counter and waited in line until a message came over the speaker system.

"Will Miss Frieda Friedman please pick up the nearest Eastern courtesy phone?"

Ann went to a nearby phone, picked it up, said something, listened briefly as she watched the departures/arrivals board, then hung up. She returned to the counter, had a ticket validated, proceeded toward the Eastern gates.

Twice Steve thought he'd lost her, but both times caught sight of the coat again. Except the second time it was moving differently and was higher off the floor and had somebody else inside it, one of those cadaverously beautiful women who starve to be fashion models.

Cursing under his breath, Steve rushed through the nearest security check and down the hallway past the gates. He saw two more sables, also worn by model types, but no Ann. In defeat, he started back toward the main terminal and spotted the model who'd made him lose the trail.

Maybe he could cut his losses a little.

"Excuse me?"

She turned and smiled at him. She had black hair and blush makeup. "Yes?"

"I couldn't help noticing your coat. It's just the kind my wife's been looking for."

She smiled again and produced a postcard-size advertisement that proclaimed,

> FURious.
> Not just a coat.
> A way of life.
> FURious.
> Serious... sensuous... mean.
> Today's comment on today.
> And a nice comment on you.
> Not just for anyone...
> But maybe for you.
> Not just in any salon...
> But maybe in yours.

Steve looked up. "Some kind of promotion, I guess."

She only smiled.

"So what's the point of walking around here? Just waiting for someone to ask you about the coat? Not everybody's going to be as forward as me. I'm in the business." He showed her his Hershey Advertising Agency card.

"We don't depend on someone asking. If you're in the business, you'll understand."

"I get it. The idea's to build the image of the coat being worn by beautiful people."

She smiled. "Thank you."

"Great idea! Who's doing it? What agency? Who's the client?"

She referred to his card. "I'm very sorry, Mr. Hershey, but we're not allowed to give out that information."

"Uh huh. But I figure since I'm in the business..."

"Then you'll understand." She smiled, returned his card and swept away.

Now two more FURious coats popped out at him like blips on a radar screen, both gliding about on professional human forms. And then he saw another that didn't glide so much as it sauntered. It was a gait he'd learned to recognize from following it all evening. Ann moved with the deliberate speed of a girl who had no time to be accosted. This time Steve kept the coat in sight.

Until he let it disappear through the doors and outside. The problem was he got distracted for a moment. As Ann was nearing the door, she was passed by another FURious coat. And this one was worn by the charming, the beautiful, the elusive Kansas Gloria.

4

Gloria didn't see Steve. Her big blue eyes were fixed on an objective, and her blonde hair trailed out behind her at an angle that indicated she might be late. She stood in an Eastern ticket line until an announcement came over the loudspeaker for a Miss Gilda Gill. Gloria left the line and picked up the courtesy phone, then returned to the counter to have a ticket validated.

Steve kept his eye on her crowning glory, not the coat, as he followed her through security and to Gate Five where Flight Twenty-six had just arrived from Miami. She read the arrival board behind the check-in desk, then went into a nearby ladies room.

A moment later, a FURious coat came out, but this one didn't distract Steve. The lady was about Gloria's height, but the hair was brown and pulled straight back in a bun. The face wasn't anything like Gloria's either; it was long, attractively horsey and deeply suntanned.

Another moment, and Gloria came out. She proceeded back toward the main terminal, looking a little like she was carrying the weight of Manhattan, if not the world, on her shoulders.

Steve's cab was waiting close to where he left it, and the driver was at sixes and sevens. "Hey, she came out already. I saw her. She's gone. You lost her."

"Never mind. Follow *that* one." Steve pointed to Gloria who was ducking to enter a checker.

"Now wait a minute. Are you on the level or not? First you give me a song-and-dance about your girlfriend, like it's a lonelyhearts thing, and now . . ."

"Trust me."

"But we're probably going right back to Manhattan now. And then who knows where?"

"There!" Steve opened his wallet under the driver's nose. "Take it all! All of it!"

"Hey, I don't know you well enough to go reaching into your wallet."

"Take it, damn it! And shut up!"

"I'm only doing this to ease the pressure, understand?" He took the money. "You're the boss. All the way back to Manhattan if necessary. Anything else I can do for you?" He screeched the cab away from the curb in pursuit of the checker, ignoring the hard look of the dispatcher as he went.

"Yeah," Steve said. "Two things you can do for me."

"Name them."

"Don't lose that cab is one."

"And two?"

"You're going to have to pay the toll."

The checker led them back to the same part of the London Terrace complex where Steve had received that uncomfortable interrogation by the ex-cop doorman. Steve hit the upholstery of the front seat, an emphatic eureka. The driver flinched, turned in his seat and raised his hands to a karate position. Steve reassured him. "That's it. You're off the hook."

"I can go home now?"

"Yeah. Buy your roommate a fur coat."

"He doesn't deserve it."

"Buy yourself one then."

"What about you?"

"I don't look good in fur."

"I mean how're you going to get home?" Real concern all of a sudden.

"I live near here. I'll walk."

"Let me take you."

Steve got out. "I'm not going yet."

"Let me give you carfare." The driver leaned over and rolled down the window on the street side. "You hear me?"

"I said I'd walk."

"Okay, you're the boss. Thanks a lot. It's been real." He shoved a business card through the window. "This tailing stuff, I could really get into it. Here, take my card."

Steve did. "Even cab drivers have them?"

"If you get anymore expensive urges, give me a call. Or maybe we could have lunch."

Steve shoved the card in his pocket and walked toward the building without so much as a goodbye to the driver with whom he'd formed a relationship.

His nemesis had been replaced by a new doorman, a short Hispanic type.

"Excuse me," Steve apologized. "The lady who just came in . . . she's with me, but she didn't tell me what apartment."

"Pardon?"

Steve said the same thing very slowly. He pantomimed a lady in a fur coat. He tried to pantomime the movement of the coat.

A light lit in the doorman's face. "Ah!"

"What apartment?"

"Pardon?"

Steve showed him the list in his notebook. The man was better at reading than hearing English, and he shook his head at each name until Steve pointed to "Harry Maloney." Then the doorman beamed with pride.

Steve was relieved and grateful. "Thank you. *Gracias.*"

"Furs," the doorman smiled. "Maloney furs. Nice man."

Steve took the elevator to the tenth floor and went to the door of 10-H. Any voices that might have been inside were muffled by a stereo playing classical music. The knob turned, and Steve darted to a stairway exit and hid behind the door. He heard the Maloney door open and Ann's voice saying, "It's just that I don't want any hard feelings, you understand. Check it out, and I'll come back Monday."

A masculine mumble, indistinguishable.

Then a voice that sounded like Gloria's. "Don't worry, Ann."

The door closed and footsteps faded toward the elevators. Steve looked out and saw a now-furless Ann getting on the elevator. Feeling confident Gloria was going to stay, Steve walked down two floors and caught the elevator there.

Now he had a name to get Big Moe off his back. He should have been relieved. But, if anything, maybe he felt a little worse. He had a whole lot more than a name now, and he didn't understand what it added up to. He didn't like leaving puzzles unsolved.

5

Saturday, April 21

There was clean sweat and dirty sweat. The clean type came from honest physical exercise and was practically odorless until it hung in a locker for a couple of days. The other kind came from nervousness, armpit stuff. Running or pumping iron, when not in competition, produced clean sweat. Steve had been running. He had pushed beyond his four-mile limit and decided to do another twenty laps around the gym track. When he felt himself getting tired, he got angry, and that gave him the energy he needed to reach his new goal. It also cleared his mind. Clean sweat. Now he was in the sauna and having one hell of a dirty kind because the image of Big Moe was back in his head.

The easiest thing would be to tell Moe that Harold Fancher was an alias for a fur man named Harry Maloney who lived on the corner of

Twenty-fourth and Tenth, and that was probably where Gloria spent her spare time. Then Steve could back off and let nature take its course. Then probably somebody would get killed. Moe or Maloney. Maybe both. Moe was certainly capable of violence, as Steve had recently discovered. And if Maloney *was* Mafia... well, those guys were known to be immature and hold grudges forever.

The Mafia was insidious, too. For all Steve knew, the two guys in the sauna with him... they were steam room types... they were ugly enough. Then one of them mentioned FURious, and they turned out to be in the garment trade.

"Y'see, the world steps aside for an idea whose time has come," one of them pontificated.

"Yeah, ain't it the truth?" asked the second banana. "I tell you, you can sell anything if you get the right angle on it."

"Y'see, that's what I've been saying all along. What's so special about the thing itself. You know what I mean?"

"Yeah, it's just..."

"I mean, what is it? Sure, it's sable, and sable is not what you'd call cheap. But the coats are all the same. Why should anyone want to lay out thirty or forty thousand to own what amounts to a copy?"

"Well, a Rolls Royce is a copy."

"That's what I've been telling you. They're going after the FURious as a status symbol... A. And B, a status symbol shared by knockouts. They're not marketing a *fur*. They're marketing an *idea*, understand? It's chic. It makes you a member of a club. And it's got that air of mystery besides. You still can't buy one. Nobody knows how to get one. I tell you, they're gonna stretch this thing until the consumers are drooling. It'll sell out as soon as it hits the market. By the time the fad wears off, somebody's gonna make a big killing."

"You kow who's behind it?"

"You kidding? The image itself is so strong, nobody . . . no consumer . . . even gives a damn about that. All they can see is the coat."

"Nobody in the business?"

"Nobody in the business, either. It's one of the best kept secrets since they started hiding cases of Canadian Club."

The conversation turned to other classic promotions, and Steve stopped listening. He bravely moved the towel from between his gluteus maximi and the wooden bench, eased himself down and wiped the dirty sweat from around his eyes. As usual, the thing that was really rough was the pressure. Big Moe's "tomorrow" still rested heavily, and that toorrow was today. Maybe Steve could avoid him by staying in the sauna and melting down into a less recognizable form.

He felt a rush of cold air. Moe stood in the doorway, eyes wide and expectant. "Why'nt'cha tell me where you was gonna be?"

"Oh, didn't I?"

One of the garment men looked up angrily. "Hey!" Then he saw Big Moe. "Say, would you mind closing the door, please? Give us a break. You're letting out the steam."

"What's the scoop?" Moe asked Steve, impervious to the grief he was causing.

"Not here," Steve whispered. He left the small, steamy room, closing the door behind him. "You showering?"

"Naw, I couldn't even work out today."

"Mind if I do?"

"I'll wait."

Steve figured it out in the shower. He'd continue being devious but with more authority.

When he came out, Moe hit him with the question again. "So what's the scoop?"

Steve did little rat-a-tat-tats on the air with the palms of his hands. "Shhh!" Then he put a finger to his lips, figuring Moe would get the message if it was delivered with enough variations. Steve looked furtively about, as though each naked guy in the locker room was a potential threat. Moe got caught up in the act and toddled along after Steve like a puppy who expected a crunchy treat, as Steve padded purposefully like he knew what he was doing. They sat on the bench in front of Steve's locker. Steve jerked his head to indicate that Moe should sit on the other side of him, by the wall, and the big man obeyed promptly.

Steve explained, "Sometimes there're guys who can read lips. This way nobody else can see what I'm telling you."

"Yeah." Moe was impressed.

"Now pretend like I'm just telling you how many laps I ran today. Don't get excited or you'll give the whole thing away." Steve worked the combination of his locker and made an elaborate show of being casual. "Moe, I'm not going to give you the name of the guy who's seeing Gloria." Having said that, he rushed on. "I know if I told you the guy's name, you'd go barrel-assing over to his place, and when the dust was settled, a lot of people could be dead. Remember, I told you he was Mafia. He's got friends of sorts. And this little job of yours has got me involved in a situation where my life's at stake. Now you don't want to see me getting killed over this, do you?" He paused and fished some clothes from the locker, then realized he wasn't getting an answer. "Well, *do* you?"

"I'm thinking."

"Well, think about this. It's not just my life at stake. It's Gloria, too. Whatever happens to me, I'm not going to risk her life. You didn't rescue her from Port Authority so she'd wind up dead, now did you?"

"Naw, I guess not."

"So give me another couple of days. Maybe I can work it out for you and meet the guy so no one else gets hurt."

Moe raised his voice. "I don't see . . . !"

Steve cut him off with a gesture and jerked his thumb toward a pudgy, old guy who just entered the row of lockers. Again, for emphasis, Steve put a finger to his lips. Moe got the idea, though he was obviously puzzled how the flabby old guy could be a threat to anyone.

"You've got to trust me, Moe. Now do you or don't you?"

"Yeah, sure, Steve."

"There's just one other thing." Steve thought he could intimidate Moe further by asking for a lot of money. "I've had to lay out a lot of cash on this case, and I need a couple hundred to cover expenses."

Moe pulled a wad of bills out of his pants pocket and peeled off four fifties. Steve was stunned by the liquid assets, especially compared to the way Moe lived, in that seedy apartment of his. But this was no time to ask about that.

When they reached the sidewalk outside the Y, the big man reluctantly turned east and Steve started west. As he walked away, Steve felt relieved, then lonely, then closer to the pavement than usual.

6

Sunday, April 22

Steve spent the next day with Jody Stewart at her studio apartment on the Upper West Side, an oasis from his work, problems and weekly routines.

They had been "seeing each other," as the expression goes, for almost a year. By now the room was peppered with artifacts of their relationship. The sleep sofa with the wine stain from the time Steve got amorous and careless. The framed eight-by-ten glossy of Steve which he used professionally and on which he'd scrawled their little joke, "To Jody. You were swell!" There was a small Sony television set which they seldom watched anymore, not since the time she decided he was watching too many late shows and the set had become a rival for his affections, and she'd written "Off Limits!!" in lipstick on its beige plastic side. All of these things gladdened Steve's heart.

There were other things he merely tolerated.
The insidious smell of incense. And the Sunday
Times which Steve plowed through with a sense
of duty but which he always approached with a
vague apprehension.

This Sunday he ignored the *Times*. The oasis
was more important. Their first springtime
together was more important. The eggs Benedict
were more important. Jody was more important.

She was the kind of girl who was pretty now
and would be beautiful by the time she got to be
an old lady. She had long brown hair that hung
straight to her shoulder blades, small but
piercing brown eyes, acceptable breasts on a nice
figure. She was much younger but only an inch
taller than Steve.

Four years ago, Jody had a difference of
opinion with her mother, a more socially conscious person, back home in Chicago. They had
different ideas about what proper young ladies
should do with their lives. So Jody packed up her
portable typewriter and took off for Manhattan
without a word or forwarding address. Mrs.
Stewart didn't become really worried until her
daughter appeared on the late news as part of a
feminist rally in Manhattan's Union Square.
Mom picked Steve's name out of a Manhattan
Yellow Pages and asked him to find the daughter
who had gone astray and looked undernourished
and was poorly dressed. When Steve found Jody,
she begged him not to tell her mother, who could
be a terrible pest. Steve had been feeling tender
and, by the time they'd worked something out, he
and Jody had a relationship started.

Now Jody was pursuing an unsuccessful
career as a writer. She wrote poetic novels about
young ladies who had trouble relating to their
mothers. So far, she was only regarded as a great

literary talent among her friends, mostly women who had trouble relating to their mothers. Steve once tried to convince her that she should turn her talents to more commercial stuff. For instance, she was throwing over a great chance to use his knowledge about the detective game. But, having made the transition from waffle to New Yorker with only occasional relapses, she didn't want to deal with the seamier sides of the city, and she wasn't about to sacrifice her art for a fast buck writing private eye stories.

Besides her writing and Steve, Jody had another great interest in life, and that's what the incense smell was all about. She called it her "path of enlightenment." Once a week, she picked up incense and attended "classes" at FREE (The Foundation for Rehabilitation, Education and Enlightenment) down in the Village. Steve wasn't absolutely certain what went on there, but he had taken the trouble to find out it didn't involve group gropes, those sessions he'd heard about where people in leotards felt each other up to communicate with each other's spirit. Though still a little leery about FREE, he was always reassured by Jody's air of purity, a quality which gave an extra kick to their love making. Some other side benefits of Jody's path were the way she could deal with pressure by sidestepping, whenever she chose, into a beautiful tranquility and, no less important, the way she brought more and more magic to her cooking, like the eggs Benedict.

Steve raised his bloody Mary in salute to this Sunday's offering. She raised her virgin Mary (FREE didn't believe in alcohol), and they clinked glasses. Steve did his imitation of other people imitating Bogart. "Here's looking at *you*, kid."

He wondered if Jody could hold her own

with those models at Kennedy and decided she probably could. Except, to her mother's despair, Jody almost always dressed casually. "You know something, kid?" he continued the bad imitation. "I hardly ever see you in something fancy. You ever worn a fur?"

She frowned. "Cancel cancel." It was an expression she'd picked up on her road to enlightenment. It was reputed to be computer language used to erase errors. Jody explained that the mind was a computer and that you behaved as you did, were happy or sad, positive or negative in outlook, depending on what you told yourself was true or whatever you let other people tell you.

"Cancel cancel you in a fur?" he asked.

"You bet cancel cancel. I don't even want to think of myself in one."

"How come?"

"Same reason I'm a vegetarian." Her eggs Benedict didn't have Canadian bacon like his. "It just isn't necessary for animals to be slaughtered for my warmth or nutrition."

"But you don't mind that I eat meat or wear leather shoes."

"Hey, I wish you didn't, but that's your business. I've got to give you your space just like you give me mine."

"Would you like me any better, though, if I was a vegetarian?"

She shrugged. "It wouldn't hurt."

"You don't mind talking about it."

"I think we should talk about it."

Steve reached inside the jacket he'd draped over the back of his chair and got out the FURious card. "Know anything about this?"

She looked at the card, then slapped it face down on the table. Steve's fork rattled against his plate. "I know I'm against it," she said.

"You're against it."

"We all are at FREE. Mr. Smith is organizing a movement."

"He's the guy ... ?"

"The head of FREE."

"And he's organizing a movement?"

"Steve, it's bad enough to wear furs in the winter. But this FURious gimmick has *no* redeeming qualities. They're killing helpless animals to manufacture status symbols."

"Think it'll ever amount to anything?"

"Wait a minute!" She found a couple of fashion magazines, the kind she wouldn't have in the house, but Christmas gift subscriptions from her mother was one of the compromises they finally worked out. "Look at this!" Jody found an ad in each magazine.

Each showed a beautiful model in a FURious, backed by plainer ladies in cloth coats, and the copy was similar to what was on the advertising card from Kennedy.

"Once upon a time," Jody said, "the world was having its consciousness raised about not buying furs. But *now*! ..." She took a deep breath to calm her anger. "Now," she continued from her center of tranquility, "they're building a strong image, so strong that people are forgetting animals have to die."

He tried to comfort her. "Sables aren't as cute as seals."

It didn't help. "*Every* life is precious!"

He was about to hand the magazines back when something caught his eye. The pictures were identical except for one small detail. At a particular spot among the cloth coats, the person changed. In one ad the model was Ann Brewer ("Have you ever done any modeling?" "Nothing to speak of . . . just Mickey Mouse stuff.") and in the other ad it was Gloria.

He tore them out and stuffed them in his jacket pocket.

Jody thought Steve was unusually preoccupied for the rest of the day, and eventually she retreated into her tranquil mode to give him space. She only came out of it when he was leaving.

"Steve!" It was close to a scream.

"What? What?"

"Don't do it!"

"Don't do what?"

She was irritable. "Well, I don't know! But just now I got a bad premonition. Cancel cancel."

"Cancel cancel," he repeated. Her premonitions gave him the willies.

"I read somewhere," he told her, "that people who stand less than five foot nine live longer than taller people."

"I know the statistics," she said, but still looked troubled.

He went back and kissed her, a long slow kiss in case it was the big goodbye. But not premonition was going to stop him.

Detain him maybe.

He didn't leave that day, after all. But, the next morning, he carried the weight of her premonition away with him.

7

Monday, April 23

The ex-cop doorman saw Steve coming and rubbed his hands in fiendish anticipation. He even had a cynical twist around his mouth. You could see him flexing his muscles in an isometric way beneath the uniform jacket, priming himself to do a third degree on Steve. "Do we know who it is we want to see today?"

Steve countered with rough and business-like. "Harry Maloney. He in?"

"Are we expected?"

"No, I'm not. I don't know about you. Tell him it's a friend of Ann Brewer."

"Well, if you're not expected, I don't think Mr. Maloney wants to be disturbed. It's pretty early for him."

"What are you? A doorman or a private secretary?"

"Don't get smart, buster."

"The name's Steve Hershey." He handed

over one of his legitimate cards. Some cops didn't like private detectives, so some ex-cops probably felt the same way, and this one seemed to be one of them. Steve accelerated his offensive. "Come on, I don't have all day. If I don't get to see Maloney right away, he might take exception. Could be something he'd hold against you in eight months."

The doorman sneered. "Eight months?"

"Christmastime, buster!"

That did it. "All right, all right. Keep your shirt on. The only reason I held off is I think the man's under the weather right now."

"Meaning?"

"There's times he don't like to see people."

"The other doorman, the Spanish guy, seemed to think Maloney was okay."

"Well, sure. Maloney doesn't wait till Christmas to remember the little guy. Once in a while he'll bring us coffee-and when there's a chill in the air."

"Coffee and what?"

"And a little something in it, but don't say I told you so." He regretted it as soon as he said it. But too late.

Steve pressed his advantage. "Okay. Let's go."

The doorman called upstairs. He got nervous about letting it ring so long. "Hope to hell I'm not waking him up." Finally, there was a response on the other end. After some explanations about Steve ("There's a private detective wants to see you."), the doorman hung up, shrugged like Pontius Pilate and told Steve, "Ten-H."

The door to 10-H was ajar and the classical music was playing beyond it. Steve rang the bell twice before he heard shuffling movements, like a heavy man in carpet slippers. The steps paused at the door, the doorknob rattled impotently for a moment, and finally the door opened.

Harry Maloney was, like most men, taller than Steve, but by ordinary standards, short and stocky. He had a paunch like the fat man inside him was trying to get out. He had a salt-and-pepper beard, full and short, that hid half his puffy face but accentuated his small bleary eyes. The eyes said he'd either been crying or was drunk, or even both. It took some time for those eyes to focus on Steve and some time longer before anythng registered behind them.

"Huh?" A gravelly voice almost, a little mellower than that.

"Mr. Maloney?"

He considered the question. "Huh," he said finally.

"I'm Steve Hershey, and I have some information that could be important to you. May I come in?"

Maloney stepped aside, and Steve entered through a small hallway kitchen. Dirty dishes, clutter. Clutter thrived in the large living room beyond, too, and made the expensive furniture look shabby. Nothing like you'd expect for a big-deal fur man who supposedly had a thing going with Kansas Gloria.

A magnum Jack Daniels bottle, about a liter gone, was on the coffee table. So Maloney's almost-gravelly voice was charcoal filtered like the JD.

"Glad you're here." Maloney was having a spasm of consciousness after his trip to the door. "Don't like drinking alone."

"No, thanks."

"Oh, come on. You got to drink with me. This is a wake . . . what's your name?"

"Steve Hershey."

Maloney got up and turned down the stereo. "Sorry. I keep it going to drown out the kids upstairs. They play bilge. Bass sounds come right through the ceiling. It's making the paint peel." He had to think a moment. "Oh . . . the name . . . I didn't hear."

"Steve Hershey."

Maloney saw the critical look in Steve's eyes and hastened to contradict it. "I'm no drunk. But this is what you have to do at times like these. Ah, the things we do for people."

"Yeah, I know what you mean," Steve said, but he didn't. He had Maloney pegged somewhere between the second stage of intoxication (dizzy and delightful) and the third (drunk and disorderly). Like most experienced drunks, Maloney consciously worked to pull himself together, speaking and moving with exaggerated care.

"Got so many old friends in this rotten city. Always trouble for them. Always lots of trouble in this rotten apple we live in. Got to drink with my poor friends, don't I? Ah," he shook his head regretfully, "the things we have to do. So help me out. Have a drink? You like this stuff?"

Steve answered in the affirmative to the last question and it was taken as an answer to both, so he was soon holding half a tumbler of the golden-brown liquid that he normally wouldn't afford for himself. He sipped, nodded sorrowfully and pretended to take on his share of whatever was troubling Maloney.

"I'm a beer man myself," Maloney said. "Don't believe in the hard stuff. The things we have to do . . ." He trailed off into a private reverie. When he came back, he said, "Bet you've got your share of miseries, too."

"Definitely! That's why I'm here."

"Thought so. Drink up." He did, and Steve sipped. Maloney poured himself another. "I'll drink to your problems... what's your name?"

"Hershey... like the candy bar. Steve."

"Drink to your problems, Steve. Least I can do, liver be damned."

"Right." (Cancel cancel.) "Liver be damned. Now, Mr. Maloney..."

"Harry. If we're going to drink together, you got to call me Harry. Insist."

"Harry it is."

"Good. Drink up."

"Before I get drunk with you, Harry, I've got to make something clear."

"Shoot."

"I've come here, Harry, to try to avoid a murder."

Harry broke into sobs and pulled a dirty handkerchief from his hip pocket. "God, the things we have to do..."

"I have this friend whose girl friend comes here, and my friend is after your ass."

Harry listened with studied care.

"And I know," Steve said, "that you guys would wind up killing each other one way or another. So I've come here to see if we can't avoid the bloodshed somehow."

"I'm with you... Steve."

"Great! That's great! Now what I think is that the girl friend can probably settle the matter without you two guys locking horns over it. Maybe you could talk to the girl or something."

"Right, Steve. Who's the girl?"

"Her name is Gloria Emery."

"Gloria..." His eyes misted again, and he wiped them with the handkerchief.

"So will you talk to her?"

"She won't talk to me."

"Then I'll try. In fact, maybe the three of us should sit down together and map out a strategy. Maybe I can come back when she's here."

"She's here now."

"What? Where?"

"Bedroom. Won't talk to me."

"Have you had a fight?"

"Never did." He went back into his reverie. Only the arm that lifted his glass remained in the present.

"Harry!" Steve raised his voice to permeate the pickled brain. "Harry!"

"Huh?"

"Can we talk to her now? I mean, is she asleep?"

"Don't know."

"Where's...?" Steve decided not to tax Harry further. The bedroom was easily found through a hallway off the kitchen. The minute Steve opened the door, he realized how drunk Maloney really was. The mop of hair on the pillow was brown not blonde. Steve closed the door quietly and returned to the living room where Maloney was pouring himself another several shots of JD with one shaky hand and wiping his eyes with the other.

"Harry, that isn't Gloria in there."

"Not Gloria?" Harry heaved a heavy sigh and began to make noises that were somewhere between laughter and tears. "I been drinking for nothing? Not Gloria? Well, that calls for a celebration. Have another, Steve."

Steve sat down with his drink. "When will Gloria be here?"

"Don't know yet. Forget."

"Tell me, Harry..." Steve paused to see if he had the man's attention. "Are you behind this FURious campaign?"

"Can't talk about that, Steve. Strategy."

"Well, can you tell me what Gloria's got to do with it?"

"Strategy, Steve. People'd be mad at me if I talked about it." With that he passed on to the dead drunk stage, his head drooping in unconsciousness.

In repose, Maloney was even more unattractive than when conscious. Spittle drooled from his hanging head, over his beard and onto his lap. It could be neither love nor lust that tied Gloria to this derelict. Whatever their relationship was, it had to revolve around FURious. And yet, Maloney being a part of that didn't make sense either, unless he was a buffer, part of an organized-crime stooge layer designed to conceal a ringleader. Was this fur promotion a crime in disguise? One thing was clear: if there were going to be any answers, they weren't going to come from Steve's somnolent drinking buddy.

Steve propped Harry in his chair so he wouldn't keel over and hit his head on the coffee table. When he got to the door, he paused with his hand on the knob. Sometimes, like now, he reminded himself of Peter Falk as Columbo, the TV detective, who was always starting to go, stopping at a door, then turning back with a new idea. Might it not be useful later to know who was sleeping in Maloney's bed now?

He went back to the bedroom, opened the door and said "Excuse me . . ." The lady refused to wake up. So he walked quietly into the room and around to the other side of the bed. The face was partly buried in the pillow. He tried again. "Excuse me." No movement. So he put his hand on the pillow and depressed it to see the face better. The girl's eyes were wide open. But she was not awake. He knew she never would be again. And he knew that he didn't have to worry anymore about not really having a modeling job for Ann Brewer.

8

Most things were above eye level for Steve, and he looked up more than the average New Yorker. This perspective magnified his outlook. Events took on added importance, and the moments of life often built to climaxes. Surprises were routine. A dead girl in Harry Maloney's bed? Why not?

But a dead Ann Brewer?

It would have been more appropriate if the victim had been Gloria with her shady connections to Maloney on one side and the threat of Moe on the other. But not Ann.

The phone was dead, too. It had been ripped out of the wall. So the gumshoe had to hotfoot it outside to call the police. Since Steve's office was also in this precinct, he'd had dealings with the boys at the Tenth before, and he'd earned himself some friends and a decent reputation. But he'd never been near the scene of a murder before, and he knew he'd be in for a shitload of questions this time.

He waited outside the building until the squad car came. One of the cops was an oldtimer called Ted. The other was a kid fresh out of the Academy, new to Steve.

Steve led the blue duo up to the apartment. At first, the kid thought Harry was the victim, so far gone that he didn't respond to slaps on the cheeks. But the noisy breathing and the smells that came with it told the real story.

The kid kept working on Harry while Steve showed Ted to the bedroom. By the time the kid had given up and got to the bedroom, he found his partner looking skeptically at Steve. Steve was looking at the bed. The unusual thing was that there was nothing unusual. The bed was neatly made and there was no sign anyone had ever been in it.

Ted folded his arms across his chest. "How much of that juice did you have yourself, Steve?" Since Steve seemed unable to say anything to that, Ted encouraged him with something standard about starting at the beginning, and Steve tiptoed carefully through his story as he remembered it.

Ted left his partner in charge of the apartment while he and Steve checked to see if anyone had been seen leaving Maloney's within the last ten minutes. The neighbors didn't know anything, and the doorman—now more respectful of Steve since he was in the company of a working cop—didn't know much either, but wished to hell he did. No one had left the building since Steve. Only a cleaning woman who stayed on the elevator after it stopped at the lobby, buzzed its warning and waited to be sent to the basement. Ted wanted that explained.

"Oh, you know," the doorman said. "Security. It's rigged so nobody can get to the basement without me knowing. If I don't turn the key over there, the elevator won't go any lower."

"Same thing coming up?"

"Right. Elevator stops here at the lobby so I can check it out first, see who's on it."

"Who's this cleaning lady who went down?"

"Oh, she's okay. She's known in the building. Worked for Maloney here, and I think for somebody on the Ninth Avenue end. She was just taking a sack of laundry down like she always does. Her second trip today."

"How big was the sack?"

"Which time?"

"The last time."

The doorman was expansive. "Oh, geez, like so." He spread his arms wide.

"Get us down to that basement!" Ted barked.

The doorman turned his key by the elevator, the doors opened, and Steve went down with Ted. They followed the arrows through the tunnel to the laundromat. They only found a fragile grandmother who needed a shopping cart to bring her small load to the cellar. Someone had been leaving when she arrived about forty-five minutes ago, but nobody had been there since.

Outside the laundromat, Steve and Ted looked down the corridor stretching a long city block. "Whoever it was," Ted said, "must be long gone by now."

Back in Maloney's living room, the kid was plying Harry with black coffee. The interview soon moved to the bathroom where Harry vomited away his troubles and his memory. He acted like the type of drunk who wakes up the next day and says, "Oh, wow, I must've been plastered last night. What did I do? I don't remember a thing." Harry did manage to dredge up some fuzzy recollection of a girl named Ann Brewer but couldn't remember why the name rang a bell. He didn't remember anybody being in his bed that day, alive or dead.

"You might as well let it go," Ted told Steve. "We'll get in touch if there's ever anything to talk about." Ted was a good cop but, like most, overworked. Alarms that turned out to be false could be a relief on a bad day.

"I don't know." Steve shook his head. "Seems as though we ought to get a lab man in here ... or something." He was looking for a brown hair on the pillow.

"For what?!" asked the kid. "Where's the *corpus delicti*?"

Ted nodded approvingly, then told Steve, "That's the point. Where's the body? You say there was one. Maloney says 'Huh?' For all we know, if there was a lady, she wasn't dead. She might've just woke up and walked away by herself."

"Without being seen by the doorman?" Steve asked.

"Maybe she's visiting another apartment."

"What about the phone being ripped out?"

"A misdemeanor at best."

Steve gave up his search. The pillow was clean. "Then that's that, is it?"

"Unless a body turns up or this Ann Brewer is reported missing."

When they got outside, Steve declined a ride in the squad car. He wanted to walk and think things out.

An old song kept running through his mind. "I Ain't Got Nobody" turned into "I Ain't Got No Body," background music to his jumbled thoughts. Questions just led to more questions. While his head was trying to sort them out, his feet were on automatic pilot and took him to Rothstein Printing. He went up to the offices and asked to see Ann Brewer. She'd called in sick that morning. How about Gloria? Same story. Might be a bug that's been going around.

His feet took him to Ann's apartment building. The doorman, remembering the five dollar tip, smiled to see him again. "Your lady friend got her purse back."

"Yeah, thanks. But she called in sick to work this morning, and I'm worried about her."

The doorman rang the apartment, and there was no answer. Steve said he had a key, and the doorman let him go up. Steve found a skeleton key that worked and let himself in. He checked out all the rooms. Nobody was there. No body either.

The apartment was neat as a pin. It had a lot of mirrors, like Ann needed reassurance she existed or something. Steve saw his own reflection—a haunted look—a confrontation with the guilt of feeling responsible for Ann's death.

He turned away from the mirrors and that didn't help. Then he saw the pictures, lots of them, all of Ann. One of her looking pretty with a man who was probably her father. Ann on a tennis court, one bare leg slightly forward in a studied pose. Ann outside Rothstein Printing with Gloria. The pictures she chose to surround herself with were those in which she looked her best.

But there wasn't one of Ann in a FURious.

And there weren't any pictures of Ann taken in her own apartment, a kind of mute testimony to the solitary life she led in a place where no one came to take a picture.

All the way back to his office, Steve fought to get the images of Ann out of his mind. He had just about succeeded when he opened his office door and saw Ann slumped over his desk and just as dead as she'd ever been.

9

Steve knew both Homicide detectives.

The one in charge was named Broderick, so Steve once called him Crawford, after Broderick Crawford, the actor who'd played his share of cops in the movies, and it caught on. But actually this Crawford looked more like the actor who wisecracked out of the side of his mouth playing tough-guy newspaper reporters, James Gleason. Crawford's new found irritability only accentuated the image.

"Now what in the hell was your relationship with this girl, Steve?" He scratched his cocked head like Gleason.

"I just met her in a bar Friday night."

"That's just great."

"And I tailed her."

"Just great."

The other detective was, so he claimed, a Mohawk Indian. Tall, well-built, short black hair, a ready smile. Since he always called his partner

Crawford, he had to put up with being called Tonto. His real name was George Fox.

"It grieves me to say so, Crawford," Tonto said, "but the record has to show our friend is a prime suspect."

The office got further crowded with a medical examiner, a lab technician and a photographer. After they'd performed their duties and Ann had been labeled with a ninety-five tag for the morgue, Steve had just about talked himself out. Except for one detail. "Put the cuffs on me."

"Oh, come on!" Crawford was testy. "You're not going to lose me my pension by running away." He was near retirement.

"No, but I've got a gut feeling. If I'm walking out of here with you, I'd better have the cuffs on. This body has been elsewhere dead. Maybe it wound up here to warn me to back off..."

"You think you're being watched..." Tonto said.

"...And I don't want it to look like I'm buddies with the cops. So put the cuffs on me, lead me to the house and lock me up for the night. I'll call my lawyer for good measure."

He didn't feel any safer when he got to the station house. He insisted he only get the one phone call he was allowed, and he used it to call Jody.

"I knew it!" she said.

"Don't get upset, Jody. It's routine."

"Then why are they keeping you there?"

"I'll explain later. Call Bill Thompson and..."

"Why do you need a lawyer if it's just routine?"

"Trust me. Call Thompson and ask him to come here looking official as hell about noon tomorrow."

"That's all? Doesn't he have to do anything else?"

"That's all."

They put him in the cage for the night to make it look good.

Tuesday, April 24

The next morning, Steve met with Crawford and Tonto over coffee in an interrogation room. Crawford said, "You keep a neat office, Steve." It didn't sound like a compliment.

"Well, it's dirty but orderly."

"No prints we could find except yours." He seemed mad about it.

"Well, somebody was there. Ann was in no condition to walk in by herself."

"*No shit*!?" He took a deep breath, then a swallow of coffee. "The lividity showed she died in a different position than we found her. So we know she was moved. Which brings us to the cleaning lady. We found out she hasn't been working the London Terrace complex all that long. Maybe two or three months." He spread out a diagram on the table. "We got this building plan from the landlord. Now the place has fourteen street entrances with fourteen separate doormen. The lady in question worked for Maloney who lives in this section, the Tower on the corner of Twenty-fourth and Tenth. She also works for another guy way over here." His finger moved diagonally to the opposite side of the ground plan. "Here at Twenty-third and Ninth. She was known by the doormen in both places. Now, the only way you can get from one section to the other is through the basement. We know the lady took two loads of something from

Maloney's building, and was seen leaving with at least one of those loads at the other end of the building."

Steve traced with his finger on the diagram. "Then this lady went to Maloney's apartment while I was out phoning the police, took Ann's body in the laundry sack down the elevator to the basement, lugged it through the tunnel to the other end of the building..."

"... Came up the elevator there," Tonto said, "and carried the bundle outside and away to your office a couple blocks away."

"But nobody saw her in my building?"

"No."

Tonto drummed his fingers on the table. "Wouldn't be the first time."

"First time what?!" Crawford snapped.

"That something happened without being seen."

"No shit? Well, that must be what happened then."

"He's having his period," Tonto explained to Steve.

Crawford ignored the comment. "We talked to the other guy she worked for, guy named Thursh. He's going to look at mug shots today. If that comes up zero, we'll have an artist draw from Thursh's description."

"Did Thursh ever think the cleaning lady was suspicious?" Steve asked.

"Not in so many words. He's the fastidious type. Wears white, wants you to take off your shoes before you go in the apartment. We talked to him in the hallway. Got the picture?"

"Yeah."

"So he thought the woman did the laundry okay but wasn't much good at cleaning. Coming from the source, that doesn't make her suspicious. He said he was thinking of getting rid of her."

"The looks of Maloney's apartment is another story."

"Anyway, Thursh said he didn't see her yesterday. And this Harry Maloney friend of yours woke up this morning without his memory."

"I'd like to ask him a few questions," Steve said, "if he's sober."

Crawford nodded cynically. "That'd be real smart. If your life's up for grabs like you think, asking Maloney questions would be real smart. Help you keep a nice low profile, wouldn't it?"

"Well, somebody better ask them."

"We've practically been doing nothing *but* asking Maloney questions. What the hell do you think we do around here?"

"What questions?" Tonto asked.

Steve turned to Tonto. "Gloria Emery and the deceased both had dealings with Maloney; what's that all about? They seem to've been tied to this FURious promotion, right? Okay, what's *that* all about?"

"We're going to see what we can get out of the models at Kennedy if they're still there," Tonto said.

"I got a better idea." Steve took the magazine ads from his jacket pocket and spread them out. "Just find out who did these. Maybe the agency can tell us why the big difference in these ads are . . ." He pointed to the dead and the missing. ". . . One's Ann Brewer and the other's Gloria Emery."

"Okay."

"Next question: How come a fur promoter like Maloney doesn't have a fancier place? How come a big-deal fur promoter is a drunk who couldn't sell shit to a fly?"

Tonto interrupted, "How come there's nothing in that apartment of his to show he's in the business in the first place? He doesn't have an office."

"Right," Steve said. "And I've seen furs come out of the building and go in, but no furs when I was there."

"Well, he's obviously..." Tonto began.

"...A middleman," Steve concluded.

Crawford pleaded, "Turn off the Steve and Tonto show, will you? Okay. We'll see what we can do for Maloney's memory. But I don't think we can hold him. Maloney's not talking, and Brewer's dead. That's all there is, there ain't no more."

"Except for Gloria Emery," Steve suggested.

"Yeah, and she's not available."

"Better find her fast."

"*Good idea*! Look! Except for her apartment, Rothstein Printing or Maloney's... and now the agency that did the magazine ads, we don't know where she might turn up... alive or dead. We want to find her, too, you know, after what you told us about the shenanigans at Kennedy."

"Well, I'm being paid to find her. Maybe I can help."

"What the hell do you want to get involved for?"

"I figure I *am* involved."

"Don't you have anything else to take your mind off it?"

"Definitely. I've got half a dozen clients cooling their heels. But I've got to do something about this."

Tonto looked at Crawford. "Certain superiors won't like it," was his parting shot as he picked up the ads and left the room.

Crawford scratched his head. "You got yourself a vendetta or something, Steve?"

"Something like that."

"Damn it, this is a damn awkward situation. If you were only on the force, we wouldn't have to walk on eggs so much."

"I like it where I am."

"Why?"

Steve shrugged. "It's better than standing with the sopranos."

"Huh?"

"Never mind."

"Haven't you found out yet you're not Sherlock Holmes?"

"And I'm not Philip Marlowe either. Mickey Spillane wouldn't use me for a semicolon."

"Well, then what's the percentage in chasing adulterers and all that crap? I just don't get it."

"If the truth were known, Crawford, neither do I."

Bill Thompson showed up, punctual as usual, at noon. He liked to talk in legal jargon to intimidate people but was an okay guy, a Brooks Brothers type with a studied professional air. He arrived ready to take a strong legal offensive against the establishment and was a little bewildered when that turned out to be unnecessary. But he landed on his feet from years of practice having Steve for a client.

"It would appear," he said, "that you require my role more than my bonafide services."

Just as Steve was leaving with his fellow actor, Tonto caught up to them. "Hang on a second, Steve..."

"What? You got my office sealed?"

"No, you can use it. That isn't it. We just got a couple late flashes."

Steve left Thompson in a neatly-pressed pose and went to another part of the hallway with Tonto.

"The Brewer girl wasn't assaulted sexually," Tonto said. "And it looks like she died of suffocation."

"I don't need an Indian to tell me that."

"Then how was it done if you're so damned smart?"

"With the pillow, I suppose."

"Explain please how a trace of animal fur found its way into her lungs."

"She was smothered with a fur coat?"

"Expensive way to go, eh?"

"Yeah," Steve nodded solemnly. "Real high class."

10

"I heard you needed a cleaning lady."

She was feather dusting the desk. She wore a flowered dress with a lace collar, and short sleeves exposing arms capable of carrying a body away from a scene of the crime. Her face was painted with rouge, her lips with cherry lipstick. Her hair was white.

"I see you're pleased." Her voice was dusky. The lipstick parted in a smile of even white teeth. She waved the feather duster at Steve, and then he noticed she was wearing pink cloth gloves. "You men are the world's worst housekeepers. I don't know what you'd do without us, do you?"

Steve opened his mouth but nothing came out.

"You men are always going off leaving the place in a mess. Awful black fingerprint powder all over everything. What do you care? You're off to some nice clean police station. Goodness me, I think you should stay home more. I really do. It isn't healthy running around so much. Did you hear on the radio? Today's air quality is unacceptable. Why, you could get killed if you're not careful."

He got the message. "I won't have to go running around all that much anymore."

"Now why is that?" She lifted a mop pail from the floor and hugged it.

"The police don't think I can be much help to them."

"Well, I'm certainly glad to hear that, Mr. Hershey. I certainly am. I'm so tickled about it, I'll tell you what, I'm not even going to charge you for my work."

"That's mighty decent of you, Miss..."

"Misses."

"Mrs...."

"No, no, no. It's Miss Misses!"

"Miss Misses? That's your name?"

She nodded. "I like you. You're short, but you're cute. Let's have a drink." She took a bottle of Hiram Walker from a desk drawer. With the mop pail handle over her arm like a purse, she poured healthy portions into two tooth glasses on the desk. Then she took a small brown envelope from the pail and poured some powder from it into one of the drinks.

It was about a gram's worth and, if it happened to be chloral hydrate, not a fatal dose.

"Try this," she said. "See if it doesn't improve the flavor."

"I'm not very thirsty."

She removed a .45 from her cornucopic pail and pointed it at Steve. She was left-handed. "Do you like this? I picked it up for a song at Macy's, on sale. I noticed you've got one in your desk a lot like it. Did you get yours at Macy's?"

Steve decided to sit down.

"No, no. Not there." She winked and gestured with the gun toward the bedroom. "Go on," she coaxed. "Here. Take your drink with you."

He took the glass and walked into the bedroom.

She indicated the bed. "Now make yourself comfortable. But be careful not to spill your drink."

The bed seemed canopied with doom as Steve got on it. She stepped up on the bed and perched on the footboard facing Steve. She crossed her right leg over her left, the way a lot of left-handed people did. "Comfy?"

"I have a girlfriend... We're practically engaged..."

"I do have your attention, don't I?" She took a sip of her drink and gestured with the gun.

"Definitely," Steve said.

"Good. Because I have an important message for you from the Cleaning Ladies' Union." Laughter. "No, no, no, it's the Cleaning Ladies' Union *East*. Get it? C-L-U-E?"

"What's the message?"

"Everybody in the Union wants to be sure you take care of your health and don't go galivanting around where you could get hurt. Do you know what kind of places I mean?"

"I think so."

"And you mustn't stick your nose in where it's not needed. Who knows? You might think you've come across something the police want. Some mysterious stranger could bring you something. Now, pay it no mind. And don't go confusing the poor policemen with it. They have enough troubles as it is, don't you think?"

"Definitely."

"Just stick to your usual clients. You've been neglecting them, haven't you?"

"Yes, I have."

"Then can I tell CLUE you'll behave yourself from now on?"

"Definitely."

"Why, that's just wonderful, Mr. Hershey." She raised her glass. "Let's drink to it."

Steve sipped obediently.

"Oh, no, no, no. That's no way for a private eye to drink bourbon. Come on now. Chug-a-lug the way you're supposed to."

He did. Whatever she'd put in the drink really didn't do anything for the flavor.

"That's real nice, Mr. Hershey. You're looking more like a private eye every minute." She sipped delicately and coughed. "My, my, I just don't know how you men put it away the way you do. Now, I don't want to be a bother to you. I know you have to go beddy-byes. You need your rest, a growing boy like you, after all you've been up to recently. So I'll just sit here and finish my drink and wait for you to go to sleep. And then I'll clean up some more and be on my way. Why, you won't even know I was here."

Steve watched her features soft-focus and become more attractive. Before she actually started looking good to him, he stopped resisting the drug and escaped the nightmare by falling asleep.

11

It was about four hours before he woke up. Then, fully rested, he was alert to the lousy way he felt. His head throbbed like the bass sounds Harry Maloney said were peeling his ceiling. An undoctored bourbon helped deaden the noise.

True to her promise, the cleaning woman had made a clean getaway. The lack of evidence was the only indication she had ever been there.

Steve spaghetti-legged his way to the telephone to report his latest hallucination. The receiver cord trailed around the phone in front of the dial. Steve never left it that way. He always picked it up with his left hand, leaving his right hand free to dial or take notes, and the cord would rest to the left of the phone after he hung up. The unusual configuration proved some left-handed intervention. She had made a call or wiped away fingerprints. Or . . .? Balancing his heavy stapler on the plungers to keep them down, Steve unscrewed the earpiece and found a small transistor receiver inside, what is known in the vernacular as a "bug." He left it where it was, screwed back the earpiece, removed the stapler and dialed the precinct.

"Tenth Precinct. Reilly."

"This is Steve Hershey. I believe you have a couple of Homicide detectives working out of the station house right now. John Broderick or George Fox?"

"Who? Oh, yeah. Just a minute, Steve."

A moment later. "Fox."

"Steve Hershey, George."

"What?"

"Am I speaking to George Fox?"

"You are. Am I speaking to Steve Hershey?"

"Yes, George. Is your partner John Broderick around?"

Steve could hear Tonto drumming his fingers near the phone. Then, "No, Stephen, John is not here at the moment. May I help you?"

"You'll recall asking me not to leave town without notifying you?" Steve asked.

More finger drumming. "Yes, Mr. Hershey! We regard it important to maintain your availability owing to your relationship to the crime."

"I have just received word that my dear aunt in Iroquois, Illinois, has taken deathly ill, and I should like to visit her, with your permission. I'm quite certain I can't tell you anything further to assist in your investigation."

"I believe we have the Iroquois number, don't we? I seem to recall you left it with us during a previous case."

"Yes, you have my number."

"When might we reach you there if necessary, Mr. Hershey?"

"I have a few loose ends to tie up here before I leave. But I should be in Iroquois by noon tomorrow."

"Very well. Inform us when you return."

As he was hanging up, there was a knock at the door. Though killers weren't normally polite enough to knock, Steve opened the bottom desk drawer to confirm that the cleaning lady had left the gun. He turned his radio on loud near the phone for the bug's benefit.

"Come in."

The door opened softly, and there was the frecklefaced kid who'd been with Ann on Friday. He was carrying a grocery bag and his eyes were wet. "Mr. Hershey?"

"Yeah."

"I . . ." He couldn't get control of himself and sank helplessly into a chair by the desk, throwing his head back in agony.

Not knowing what else to say, Steve said, "Want a drink?"

The kid shook his head no, also shaking away some of the moisture. Then he cleared his throat. "My name's Mike Ellerson. Remember? From Jeeve's?"

"Yeah."

"Could you turn the radio off, please?"

"It's stuck. Come on." Steve led the way to the bedroom. Mike sat on the edge of the bed, Steve in the chair next to it."

"I'm . . . I *was* a friend of Ann Brewer's," Mike said.

"I guess you heard."

Mike handed him the grocery bag. "Maybe I should've given this to the police when they came, but . . ." He put his head in his hands and sobbed.

Steve took a leather purse from the bag. It was the one Ann had left in the bar. Come to think of it, it also looked like the same one Ann had held in the magazine ad. It had the same oval plate under the clasp. It was empty. "Why would the police be interested in this?"

"Ann thought it was important." Mike wiped his eyes with his shirtsleeve. "She didn't tell me very much. Ann could be very secretive when she wanted to be. I know she had some pretty heavy things on her mind, though. I could tell. Then after she talked to you she brightened up a little. She told me she had a chance to be somebody..."

"When was this?"

"Friday night. Late. She came to my place. I thought..." He sighed. "But it was only to tell me about her chances and to give me the purse."

"Go on. She told you she had a chance to be somebody..."

"But she said she had to get out of something else first. I thought she meant get out of Rothstein's, but that wasn't it. Anyway, whatever it was, she said she had to do it. And I knew it was going to be dangerous."

"How did you know that?"

"Because then she gave me the purse, and she said if anything happened to her, I was to give it to you. See? If anything *happened* to her."

Steve's head tuned up the throbbing, and he rubbed his eyes hard with his palms. "Yeah."

"She said she tried to leave it with you Friday, but she wasn't thinking clearly and should've guessed you'd find some way to get it back to her."

Steve took a close look at what was etched on the silver plate, a "QO" or a "20." He asked Mike, "You know anyone with the initials Q.O.?"

"No, I don't think so."

"Would the number 20 mean anything special to Ann?"

"Not that I know of."

"Did she always carry this purse?"

"For the last few months."

"She ever say where she got it?"

"She said it'd been a gift from an admirer, but she said it like a joke. She was always joking."

"How did you find me, Mike?"

"I had your number on the card, the one you gave Ann. But you weren't here when I called, and your answering service picked up. They thought I'd dialed the wrong Hershey because they didn't recognize the name of the advertising agency on the card. So then I checked your number in the directory we have at the office. You know, one of those that lists by numbers instead of names? And here I am."

"Did you tell anyone else you were coming here?"

"No, I didn't think to."

"Well, don't tell anyone you came. What's your shoe size?"

"Huh? Nine. Why?"

Steve left the office and took the elevator to the lobby. While there he asked Herb the lobby man if he'd seen the cleaning woman leave the building. Herb, who prided himself on powers of observation, said neither leaving nor entering.

Steve went through the lobby door of the shoe repair shop.

Oscar saw him coming. "They ain't ready yet. Tomorrow."

"I bet you say that to all the fellas."

Oscar grinned. "Okay, Steve, so I'm a very busy man. You got shoes here or not? Nah, you don't, do you? I wouldn't forget those special jobs you wear."

"What I need, Oscar, is a pair of nines you

haven't fixed and that haven't been picked up in so long you've given up on them."

"If they'd been here that long, why wouldn't they be fixed?"

"Come on, Oscar. I'm a busy man, too."

Oscar found a pair of brogans buried in a pile of shoes he called his graveyard. "Suppose the guy comes for these? It's been a year and a half, but it could happen. What'll I tell him?"

Steve was already out the door. Back in the office, he put the shoes in Mike's grocery bag.

"Take this sack downstairs, Mike. Go out on the street and walk right up to the door of the shoe repair. Then stop, shake your head, like you suddenly decide it's dumb to get these ugly shoes fixed because you always hated them. Turn around, and you'll see a wire trash basket. Throw the bag in the basket like it was good riddance. Then go on wherever you're going, and don't look back. You think you can do that?"

"Sure. But why?"

"The less you know, the better. Okay?"

Mike nodded and left with the bag.

The obliging cleaning lady hadn't thrown away the trash at the bottom of the closet. Steve found a large carton and newspapers. He brought them to the desk, wrote a note to Tonto and Crawford, put the note in the purse, then packed the purse with wadded-up newspapers in the carton. He addressed the package to Crawford at the station house. Then he took the package to another office on his floor where one of his old girlfriends worked. He told her he was leaving town to visit his sick aunt in Illinois. Full of sympathy, the girl agreed to send the package out with whatever else her office was mailing that day.

When he got to the street, he saw that the

trash basket didn't hold the paper bag with the wornout shoes. He hoped that whoever took it would believe that what Mike brought out of the building was the same thing he took in. He also hoped he'd soon find out why the purse was so damned important.

12

Moe lived in one of those buildings that refused to die over on East Fourteenth between Avenues B and C. Steve had him pegged as the type who'd live there until they tore the building down around him. It was cheap, and Moe spent a lot of time in girlfriends' pads anyway.

As soon as the tired door scraped open on the third floor front apartment, Steve shot a put-upon look at Moe and demanded, "When the hell are you going to get a telephone in this dump?" Keeping Moe on the defensive might be the best way of handling him.

"Aw, Steve, I had one once, but they took it out on me." Moe had been working out and was sweating through his Y tee shirt.

"Never mind, never mind." A great sigh. "You're just not making it very easy for me to help you, that's all." Steve pushed officiously into the kitchen. "How can you live in a place like this?"

Moe's kitchen had an ancient, graying bathtub, cracked or missing linoleum, a dripping faucet, a bare lightbulb, an old refrigerator that emitted death rattles and a couple of friendly emissaries from the secret cockroach kingdom. Merely the highlights of merely the kitchen.

The next room featured on the floor a mattress that a falling-down-drunk wino would think twice about falling down drunk onto.

Sufficiently depressed, Steve kept going to the front room which was, by contrast, cheerful. A dull gray light bravely filtered its way through windows heavily sooted by the Con Ed plant farther east. The room had a wooden chair, a moth-eaten studio couch from which the moths had long since gone on to better things, and a set of fifty pound weights on the floor. The walls seemed held together by scotchtape that, only incidentally, held up newspaper clippings and snapshots of Moe in weightlifting and bodybuilding competitions, which, in turn, competed for wall space with one of those nudes painted on velvet.

Steve asked "Have you seen Gloria?"

Moe shook his head. "You?"

"You sure?"

"About what?"

"That you haven't seen Gloria!"

"No."

"You're not sure?"

"I mean, yeah. Yeah, I'm sure I haven't seen her. What are you doing, Steve, trying to confuse me or something?" He got up and started lifting the weights, expelling great air explosions with each lift.

"You haven't talked to her?"

"No. (Puff) I ain't talked to her. (Puff) You?"

"No. But I'm worried about her. We've got

ourselves a situation here. Understand what I'm telling you, Moe?"

"(Puff) Sure, Steve."

"Listen to me!" Steve got up and put his foot on the weights' bar when the weights hit the floor, putting a stop to the exercising. Moe looked up, surprised. "Listen carefully," Steve said. "Did you ever hear of a guy called Harry Maloney?"

Moe thought. "The exercise guy at the Y?"

"No, not that Harry. Harry Maloney is the one Gloria's been seeing."

Moe chewed on the name like he was hungry. "Harry..."

"Maloney."

"Maloney! Harry Maloney! Where's he live, Steve? Can I knock his head...?"

"No! Listen! This isn't a case of your girlfriend sleeping around. I don't believe Gloria ever slept with him at all."

"But you said..."

"Maloney is a stumblebum drunk, not a bit handsome, and I doubt he could even get it up."

Moe looked stupified. "But... but, Steve, I don't get it."

"You can't understand why Gloria would leave a charmer like you to spend some sexless time with a jerk like Maloney."

"Yeah! Right!"

"Well, it's because there's something *else* going on."

Steve told the story from the top, what they knew and what they didn't know. He had to tell it slowly, making sure Moe understood each point, and Moe was acting more distracted than usual.

"So," Steve concluded, "if she wasn't sleeping with him, you don't have to pound his head through the sidewalk, do you." It was a statement, not a question.

"Yeah. I mean no. I guess not."

"And the fact that Gloria's friend was murdered... well, that could mean Gloria's in danger, too. She hasn't shown up for work, and nobody knows where she is."

"Well, you leave it to me now, Steve. You done a good job. I'll take it from here."

"What do you mean?"

"I'll find Gloria. I'll protect her like I always did. Don't you worry. You're out of it now. What do I owe you?"

"I'm already in this up to my eyeballs."

"Then you just get out of it. Somebody's out to get you if you don't. Ain't that right? Ain't that what you've been telling me?"

"I didn't tell you about the pur..."

"Get out of it, Steve!" Moe broke in with surprising speed. "You hear me?! I'm telling you!"

Steve felt he was fast losing his advantage. "Oh shit! You're crazy! You know that?"

"I'm crazy in love with my little Gloria."

"You're crazy six ways to Wednesday! Here I've gone to all this trouble to make them think I'm leaving town..."

"Shut up, Steve!"

"Shut up my ass! Tomorrow I'm..."

"Shut up, Steve!" The way he said it was frightening. "Gloria's my girl, and I'll take care of her! Get me?"

"Yeah, Moe, I get you. Goodbye." Steve hurried from the room, opened a closet door by mistake and ran straight into some stinking gym suits. He turned on the light, as long as he was there, to be sure Gloria wasn't. When he turned to leave, he saw Moe's massive bulk clogging the doorframe. Moe shoved him back up against the closet wall, squeezed into the small room and shut the door. Before Steve could yell, Moe clamped his fat hand over Steve's mouth.

"I told you shut up. I got to help you do it?" In his effort to be thorough, Moe had blocked Steve's nose. "You gonna shut up now?"

Steve managed a nod because suffocation was his second least favorite way of dying, second to falling down an elevator shaft.

Moe pulled his hand back but kept it poised, ready to return if necessary. "Now don't talk, okay?"

Steve nodded.

Moe smiled. "Good." Then he waited until he remembered what he wanted to say. "Yeah." He remembered. "I want you to stay out of trouble, Steve. I got to go to Canada in a couple weeks for the competition down there."

Steve pointed up.

"Huh?"

Steve whispered, "Up. Canada's *up* there."

"Yeah. Want you to be around so you can come with me and see me win."

"But, Moe, don't you think...?"

"Shhh."

One eye on Moe's poised, sweaty palm, Steve whispered, "Don't you think Gloria's safer if we both work on this thing? I mean, there might come a time when it'd be a good idea for us both to see Maloney. You've got the muscle, but I've got the questions."

"Guess so."

"So what do you say? Partners?" Steve held out his hand, then quickly pulled it back.

"Okay, Steve. Partners." Moe lowered his palm to a handshake position.

Steve gritted his teeth and accepted Moe's grip. When he had his hand back, Steve said,

"Don't worry. I'm going to cool it while they think I'm out of town. Later on, I'll get in touch with you and tell you what we better do. You might not even have to miss that competition."

Moe shook his head. "Wouldn't want to do that. That's what pays the bills around here."

"Just promise me you won't make a move without me."

"Okay."

It was getting very close in the closet. "Can I go now?"

"Sure, Steve."

Moe clamped his hand back on Steve's mouth, once more clumsily blocking off the air. With his hand glued in place and cradling his arm around Steve's neck, Moe opened the closet door with his other hand and dragged Steve out toward the kitchen door. He opened the door and shoved Steve out into the hallway.

"Stay out of trouble," he said and closed the door in Steve's face.

Steve stood in the hallway catching his breath. He could hear Moe talking to himself inside. The son-of-a-bitch was even crazier than Steve had imagined.

13

Wednesday, April 25

The Iroquois Hotel was very near the famous Algonquin on Forty-fourth Street. Steve was fuzzy about whether the original tribes had any kind of relations with each other, but the hotels existed amicably enough. Since a few years ago when some business brought Tonto and Steve to the imposing Bar Association building across the street, "Iroquois" had been the code word for the small restaurant in the hotel, a good place for secret meetings.

Steve took the precaution of getting there five minutes before noon to secure a corner spot. But every table in the dark, lamplit room was occupied. So he stood at the bar, had an ale and waited. He noted with satisfaction that the place was still noisy when full. People who wanted to be heard were less likely to eavesdrop.

For the benefit of onlookers, Tonto greeted Steve like an old buddy he hadn't seen for a long time. Crawford skulked some distance from the effusive scene. They led Steve to a table for four that was occupied by a florid-complexioned man wearing a red necktie, with a matching red handkerchief dangling from his breast pocket.

'I hate this outfit," he said. "But I simply couldn't bring myself to wear a carnation."

The man was introduced to Steve as Arthur Greenglass, head of Greenglass Advertising Associates.

"I'm not absolutely crazy about this restaurant, either," Greenglass confided, "but I probably won't be recognized here."

Tonto told Steve, "Mr. Greenglass is in charge of the FURious ad campaign, and he prefers this meeting be on the Q.T."

Greenglass used his handkerchief to wipe his forehead. "See, I may have gotten my company involved with some questionable clients. I don't think any of my people have noticed yet, and I don't want to draw their attention to it. So I wanted to meet you gentlemen outside a police station and outside my office, and..." He hesitated.

"And what?" Crawford asked.

"*And* I don't want to risk offending my client."

"Just how would you do that?"

"By breaking our confidentiality agreement."

"I see." Crawford rubbed his chin. "Well, go on."

Greenglass bit his lower lip and looked at each of the detectives. "Yes, I guess so. That's what I'm here for, isn't it?" He considered this a moment, then went on. "We took the account several months ago."

Steve interrupted. "I didn't notice any hoopla until recently."

"Well, of course. The publicity only started appearing two months ago. But we need some lead time to plan a campaign and secure magazine spots and so forth. Although, in this instance, there wasn't all that much planning on my part. The client knew exactly what he wanted. The worst kind of client. He came with the whole thing laid out and just expected my agency to handle the details for him." Greenglass downed his martini and acted like he had no more to say. "Maybe this isn't such a good idea, after all."

"What do you mean?" Crawford asked, an edge creeping into his voice.

"Hell!" Greenglass said. "For all I know, I need my lawyer."

Crawford was feisty now. "Have you done something wrong, then, Greenglass?"

"Not to my knowledge, but..."

Steve took over. "Mr. Greenglass... Art?"

"Sure."

"Let's have another drink." Steve raised his hand and got immediate attention from a waiter. After ordering another martini for Greenglass, and then pausing a few seconds, he picked up the thread. "You know, Art—Oh gee, this may be a little bit off the track. Forgive me, fellas. —But I couldn't help thinking as you were talking there how much your business sounded like mine."

"Advertising and... private investigation?"

"Yeah, just like you seem to be describing, I have to let an occasional client have his own way. He's paying, right? If he wants shit and he's willing to pay for it..."

Greenglass nodded. "That's true. You can get into that frame of mind, especially in a cutthroat business like mine."

"Being a little flexible is just part of being a professional."

Greenglass got his martini. "I must confess, it didn't hurt the client's case any when he accepted my first figure. I had left some room for negotiation, but he didn't want to be bothered with that."

"What was his name, anyway?"

"Maloney."

"Last name, right?"

"First name . . . Jonathan, I think. We call him Mr. Maloney. Company policy."

"I know a Maloney. What does yours look like?"

"Clean cut, well dressed, good build. Dark, wavy hair. Nice voice. Very persuasive."

"No, doesn't sound like the one I know. Was anyone else involved, by the way?"

"Maloney said he represented a group of businessmen who preferred anonymity. These men had negotiated an excellent fur deal and created a unique coat. It had some kind of internal design that made it move with the body in a special way.

"He intended to sell it with a two-pronged campaign. One: we'd get extensive exposure in international fashion magazines, showing essentially the same ad always, the coat on a beautiful woman being envied by other women in cloth coats. Two: beautiful women would be seen wearing it in public to reinforce the ad campaign and let people see how the coat moved. But during the early stages, the coat wouldn't be available in stores. Maloney wanted to build product desirability so high that, by the time it actually appeared, it would be presold, an overnight success.

"Well, I pointed out he was creating a fad that would not go the distance. Furthermore, the idea would be connected to my agency. And our reputation, as well as his profits, were at stake. He said he'd worry about his profits, and I'd be responsible for my reputation. That's when he said he wanted the agency's involvement kept under wraps, at least until the coat was on the market. I'm hoping you gentlemen will do nothing to expose my involvement...?"

Crawford was gruff. "Maybe we won't have to. We'll see."

"You will do your best, I hope."

"We always do our best."

Steve nudged Tonto.

"Then was it Maloney's idea," Tonto asked, "to have the coat seen at Kennedy?"

"Airports, restaurants, the theatre. He said the models had to be sworn to secrecy. That was risky, I thought, but I'm not aware of any leaks. Now I don't expect any."

"How come?" Tonto asked.

"Their loyalty is compensated. They're getting double the usual fees, plus they get to keep the furs."

"Pretty good," Steve said. "How long does this go on?"

Greenglass shook his head and sighed. "We hit the March and April issues of key magazines. The May issues are out now with no ads at all. Nothing scheduled for the future. It doesn't make sense. But what can I do? I'm working under Maloney's instructions. The last time I talked to him, he said the campaign had to pause while he worked out a difference of opinion among his management people."

"You mean some of his people don't want the campaign to go on?"

"I don't know what else to think."

"You said you worked for an identical look in the ads."

"Yes, for the most part, even the same clarity.

Maloney examined our prints with a magnifying glass to be sure the details were sharp. I tried to convince him that the model in the fur should be in focus, and the ladies in the background should not. He said, no, the background ladies represented his customers. What can you do?"

"What was different about the ads?"

"A couple of the background ladies changed."

"What was the point in that?"

Greenglass shrugged. They were the client's girl friends, I guess. It happens. They were attractive enough, so I didn't object."

"What made you think they were girlfriends, Art?"

"The way he fussed over them during the shooting sessions. Wanting them to stand just so. You know, the kind of attention you might give to a girl you'd promised to make a star."

"And you said there were a couple of them?"

"That's all. One was a short little blonde. Very attractive. The other had dark hair, medium height, needed more reassurance."

Steve looked at Tonto, and Tonto asked, "Do you know their names, Mr. Greenglass?"

"Art. I guess we'd have them back at the office. The girls had to sign release forms."

"Were they dressed the same in each ad?"

"Yes. But they changed handbags."

Steve asked, "You mean they each had more than one?"

"Several, I think. Maloney said it was some kind of subliminal preparation for a handbag promotion he might do later."

"Did Maloney specify the magazines, too?"

"I tell you, he was simply impossible. Here, let me show you." Greenglass looked furtively around the room, then pulled a briefcase from under the table. He took out three eight-by-ten color glossies and spread them out. "Now this one," he pointed to one with Gloria in the background, "had to be in this month's *Mademoiselle*. The other two," he pointed to one with Gloria and another with Ann, "were earmarked for last month's *Glamour* and *Mademoiselle*."

Steve compared the two ads with Gloria in them. "Aren't these the same shot?"

"No." Greenglass sighed. "We had to shoot the same thing twice for two different magazines just so he could get another handbag in. Impractical. Expensive. Crazy."

"Can you get us a complete set of ads?" Tonto asked.

"No problem."

Steve asked, "How about the models at the airports?"

"What about them? The girlfriends weren't in on that, if that's what you mean."

"Did Maloney lay out that part, too?"

"*There* we had more leeway. In fact, he made a big deal out of it, pretending he respected our judgment. But he was only trying to placate us."

"*More* leeway?"

"Where and when were mostly up to us. He only asked we have models at *Kennedy* on certain dates and times."

"Do you know why?"

"Yes. He said he and his partners met with their fur suppliers frequently, and whenever a supplier flew into town, Maloney wanted him to see the coats at the airport."

"What dates?" Tonto asked.

"I'd have to get that information for you. Is there some place I can send these things ... other than the police station?"

Tonto asked Steve, "How about your office?"

Steve gave Greenglass his business card. "If

you would, Art, have the stuff left in my name with the lobby man."

Greenglass closed his briefcase. "If there are no more questions . . . ?"

Steve and Tonto exchanged glances.

"No . . ." Tonto began.

"Excuse me, officer," Crawford said. "Excuse me, Mr. Hershey. Would it be all right if I asked one little question? Mr. Greenglass . . . may *I* call you Art?"

"Certainly," Greenglass said. "Is that the question?"

"No, Art. The question is, do you know when you'll be seeing Mr. Maloney again?"

"Oh, I never know."

"Would you mind keeping us posted? Thank you, Art, You can go now, if you like."

"One small blessing," Greenglass said. "I can eat somewhere else." He picked up his briefcase and left them.

Crawford flashed a big, friendly grin. A difficult moment that was saved by the waiter who, seeing Greenglass leave, rushed over full of apologies and in fear of losing more customers. He took the orders and left to do something about them.

"Well, Mr. Stephen Hershey!" Tonto said.

"George Fox," Steve said.

"You've been bugged, right?"

"More ways than one. But whoever was listening thinks I'm out of town." Steve filled them in on his visit from the cleaning woman, and about Mike with the purse. "Did you get it yet?"

Tonto shook his head. "What do you think it's all about?"

"Don't know. But Ann Brewer must've thought it was incriminating. And they didn't change purses in those ads for the reason what's-his-name gave Greenglass."

"It's Jonathan," Crawford said, "just like Greenglass remembered. He's Harry Maloney's brother. Up until now, Harry hasn't been connected with the rackets, but we know Jonathan is. He lives on the Gold Coast."

"Huh?"

"Upper Park Avenue. He's visibly prosperous without any very visible means of support. Consorts with Mafiosi. That points to a big organization behind this FURious thing... and behind what happened to Ann Brewer. It also means this'll be a tough case to crack."

"Shit!" Steve said. "Have we gotten anything else out of brother Harry?"

"If I may quote you," Tonto said, "shit. I think the booze has rotted away his memory."

"Don't you believe it," Crawford growled.

"Is he in custody?" Steve asked.

"Look, my young friend, if we're going to start arresting people on this case, especially people who hire good lawyers, we'd better know a hell of a lot more than we do now."

"The old man's right," Tonto said. "In this case, we better not move until it's going to count."

The food arrived. When the waiter was out of earshot, Crawford asked Steve, "What about this bug in your phone?"

"It's still there."

"We'll need to work out a way of being in touch as long as your cover lasts."

"You think it won't last?"

Crawford smiled. "Well, it's not like you can walk around in a disguise, is it? Unless you know how to walk on stilts. Of course, it won't last. Who knows you're in town so far?"

"Just you guys, now Greenglass, and a client of mine."

"I give it two days."

When they left the restaurant, Steve declined a

ride and walked west on Forty-fourth while the detectives went to retrieve their car from the garage across the street. They hadn't been separated more than half a minute when Steve heard something whiz in front of his eyes and splatter off a brick wall with the sickening sound of a ricochet. Tonto ran back with his gun drawn. Steve was flat on the sidewalk. Coverless.

14

Tonto pushed Steve into the store next door. Through the plateglass window, they saw Crawford run into the Royalton Hotel across the street, his gun drawn.

There was no movement behind any of the windows of the building's eleven floors. "You'd better stay here," Tonto said. "You're the target." He ran across the street to join his partner inside the hotel.

Steve looked suspiciously at a couple of customers who were looking at him. Anybody could be in on it. Even Crawford and Tonto.

Crawford and Tonto?

Hadn't Crawford once confessed he'd been bad as a kid and thought it a lucky turn of fate he didn't end up a criminal? Now near retirement, might he have found it necessary to go on the take? Crawford was certainly bothered about something these days. If a man like him was making deals with criminals, then there was nothing to keep someone like Tonto clean either. Hadn't they both seemed to pussyfoot around the subject of Harry Maloney?

My god! What was he doing to his head? *Crawford? Tonto?*

Suppose whoever monitored Steve's phone call figured out the code. Maybe they checked out Iroquois, Illinois, found out you had to fly to Chicago first, then watched the Chicago departures. When Steve didn't show up at the airport, they figure Iroquois might be the hotel on Forty-fourth, and if Steve showed up there, it meant he talked in code, couldn't be trusted and should be eliminated.

Yet, it was hard to believe a marksman could miss such an easy shot. Was it another warning? Had Steve damn well better get his ass on the next Chicago flight?

All the fear and doubt swelled up inside him like a poisonous sponge and then, his adrenalin pumping, Steve became angry. Angrier than he got when running and he tired before he reached his goal, the anger that helped him stretch beyond his limits.

He ran across the street, into the hotel and demanded of the desk clerk, "What the hell's going on?!"

The man was frightened. "I don't know, mister. I was just standing here, these two guys came in, and ..."

"What two guys?"

"Detectives, just before you, just a couple minutes ago."

"Well, where the hell are they now?"

"Upstairs. Asked who registered in the last couple of hours and then they went up."

"Stupid ...! Is there a stairway or just the elevators?"

"Sure, we got a stairway. It's the law." He pointed to an open one near him. "And those two elevators. One of the detectives took the stairs."

It was difficult, if not impossible, to trap a man in a building like this. No would-be assassin worth his salt would take a potshot at someone accompanied by two detectives unless he had an escape plan. Crawford and Tonto were playing the longshot that the guy was an amateur and they'd be able to nab him on the same floor where he'd taken a room. Having cooled down slightly, Steve decided to stay in the lobby and watch the escape routes.

Ten minutes later, Crawford and Tonto returned. "He might've got away before Tonto came up the stairs," Crawford said. "He could've gone out the Forty-third Street side."

Tonto was on the phone calling for assistance, and Crawford went to ask some questions on the other side of the building.

Tonto hung up the phone. "They should be here in a minute. You'd better stick around, Steve. You'll be safer here."

Uniformed men appeared and began a systematic search while Tonto remained on duty in the lobby.

"You think they're after you just because you're associated with cops?" Tonto asked.

"Maybe."

"Sure there isn't something you forgot to tell us?"

"Of course I'm sure."

"Some piece of evidence maybe?"

"Just that purse I sent you."

Steve repeated his story about Mike, then remembered, "That cleaning lady said something about a mysterious stranger might bring me something. 'Pay it no mind,' she said."

"The mysterious stranger being Mike Ellerson..."

"So I made it look like I hadn't received the purse..."

"...By putting old shoes in a paper bag..."

"...And mailing the purse, so no one would see me walking out with it."

"What about that purse?"

"The only way I can figure it," Steve said, "is Ann was frightened, and the purse was some kind of insurance policy..."

"...Soemthing that would keep her alive."

"Yeah, that's why she gave it to Mike."

"So?"

"So that means, if hiding the purse was going to keep her alive, she must have told her killer about it."

"And got killed anyway?"

"Yeah."

"If it's important enough to send someone gunning for you, Steve, why wouldn't it be important enough to keep Ann alive?"

"I don't know. But I still feel they're after me because they think I have it."

"Then you better pick up your bugged phone and tell them you don't. There could be guys hunting for you all over town."

At least guy number one was still on the loose. All the police found in the Royalton was a discharged shell casing from an automatic rifle. This fact made Crawford more irritable than usual during an unpleasant drive back to Steve's office.

"We weren't too smart this time, were we?" He looked accusingly back at Steve, then across the front seat to Tonto who was driving.

Tonto kept his eyes on the road: "We played the odds and we lost."

"We *shouldn't* have lost, goddamn it!"

Steve saw a slight shrug in Tonto's shoulders,

and he changed the subject. "I've got a gut feeling."

Crawford winced. "Your gut feelings give me a bellyache."

Steve ignored this. "We don't know how this FURious business adds up, do we? We don't know how it connects to the murders."

"We don't know *if* it adds up *or* connects."

But it does, just the same. We're some guys who don't understand the connection out looking for some other guys who do. So I think we'd better not tip our hand that we're looking for a connection."

"Keep it in the background," Tonto said.

"Find out about it indirectly . . ."

"Otherwise the lid'll come down hard . . ."

". . . And we might not be able to pry it open."

"Where am I?" Crawford asked. "Back in parochial school? All this fourth-grade-recitation shit you're spouting is no different than the way we're handling Harry Maloney. Of course we can't tip our hand about what we know, don't know or what we're looking for. This original thinking is giving me a headache. What makes you guys so brilliant?"

Steve apologized, "It was just a gut feeling."

"Oh, shut up!"

At Steve's building, the lobby man Herb said he hadn't received the package from Greenglass Associates yet but he'd keep his eye out for it. Upstairs, Tonto entered the office first, then signaled Steve and Crawford inside when he was sure it was empty.

Steve called his service. "There's been a change in plans. I have to stay in the city after all. Any messages?"

"No, Mr. Hershey. It's been quiet as a tomb."

After the service hung up, Steve kept the receiver in his hand and said, "I guess the lab's still examining the purse."

"You ought to be careful what you say," Tonto said. "You could be bugged."

Crawford slumped on the sofa, silently disgusted with the charade. Steve pretended to discover the bug and removed it.

"What'd I tell you?" Tonto asked. He took it to the bathroom and put it to soaking in a sink of water, then returned.

"Now they know I don't have the purse," Steve said, "and maybe my life's worth more than the gold in my teeth."

Crawford snarled, "You think these guys carry walkie-talkies? What about some gun that didn't get the message yet? Suppose it's not even the purse they're worried about?"

"Well," Steve snapped back, "I'm not going to stay holed up here until you guys get around to solving the case!"

"So what do you want?" Crawford stood abruptly. "Police protection round the clock?"

"You keep your men working where they can do the most good. I don't want any plainclothes sweetheart. I want you guys to find out who killed Ann Brewer. I want that a hell of a lot."

"You don't have to feel responsible . . ." Tonto began.

"I *do* feel responsible! Understand, Tonto? Do you understand, Crawford? I *do* feel responsible. And I don't want to carry that weight on my shoulders one second longer than I have to! Understand?"

Tonto said, "You're acting a little crazy, Steve. It isn't true that the angels look out for crazy people."

"Well, what the angels can't do, Bertha will."

"Who the hell is Bertha?" Crawford asked.

"This is Bertha." Steve opened the desk drawer and took out the gun.

15

Bertha in a shoulder holster, Steve banged on Moe's door. He heard the gruff voice from the other side. "Yeah?"

"Steve. Let me in."

"I'm busy right now, Steve."

"Let me in, you pile of shit! Or I'm going to break the goddamn door down!"

A pause. "Keep your shirt on."

The chain lock slid off, the Segal unbolted and the door scraped open. As soon as it cracked, Steve tried to push his way in. But Moe shoved him back against the door of the opposite apartment. A baby cried inside. A man's voice a couple floors above shouted "What's all that racket down there?"

Steve shouted back, "Who the hell wants to know?"

"Awright . . . awright . . ." and a door closed.

Moe nodded solemnly. "You're mad about something, Steve."

"You're goddamn right I'm mad, Moe! You

figured that out, didn't you?"

"What're you mad about, Steve?"

"Well, Moe, I'm just a little ticked off because somebody took a shot at me a couple hours ago. And you happen to be one of the few who knew I was staying in town."

Moe looked worried. "I don't want you getting killed, Steve."

"Terrific!"

"Steve, I'll bet it was that Maloney guy. You know what we're gonna do? We're gonna go over there and . . ."

". . . And pound his head through the sidewalk. I thought we already settled that."

"That was before."

"Before what?"

"Before you got shot at. Come on. You know where he lives."

Moe rushed to the stairway and got a few steps down before Steve caught up and tugged at his shoulder. Moe turned and looked up, taking a moment to adjust to Steve's head being slightly higher than his. Steve thought this gave him an advantage if he needed it. Then he thought he saw a glimmer of intelligence pass over Moe's face. Or was it shock? Whatever it was, it threw Steve off guard long enough for Moe to body slam Steve against the steps.

A piece of wood ripped out of the bannister near them. Then another. Hugging the wall, Moe moved with surprising agility up the stairs and out of sight. Steve drew his revolver and ran up after Moe.

The metal roof door was closed and had something braced against it from the other side. As Steve was trying to open it, he heard something zing off it, maybe a rifle shot. Someone could be standing on the other side, the rifle pointed at the door Steve was trying to open. He heard an angry roar that sounded like Moe, then silence.

Inching the door open, Steve saw an old metal garbage can filled with bricks against it. Why in the hell would Moe take the time to do that with an unfriendly rifleman to think about?

A sound of scuffling came from the right. Facing that direction, Steve sidled through the door, Bertha held awkwardly in his left hand leading the way.

Moe had caught the sniper on the adjacent roof and was holding him by the throat, folding him back over the edge. Getting out of the stranglehold would've allowed the guy to catch his breath while falling seven stories, seven big ones like in the old buildings with tall ceilings.

Steve felt sick. He dropped to the roof, crawled to the edge of Moe's building and leveled Bertha in their direction. He tried not to think about the guy falling or how high up they were.

"Okay, Moe. He's covered."

Moe looked over his shoulder toward Steve. Then Steve saw that the man was still holding the rifle. Steve took careful aim, figuring Moe would step out of the way, and shouted at the sniper, "Drop it! Now!"

Maybe Moe thought the command was for him because he gave the man a shove which sent him falling off the edge of the building, his scream trailing down into silence.

Steve buried his eyes in his arm, the revolver hanging limp and useless from his hand, and he retched. He breathed deeply until the nausea diminished. Then he looked up and saw Moe swaggering toward him.

Moe was bleeding from his right deltoid, and he had a big smile on his face. "There!" he said. "Now do you trust me?"

16

By the time the ambulance arrived, it might as well have been a hearse or a garbage truck. The sniper was very dead and so was any information he might have had in his head. Now his story would have to come from fingerprints, birthmarks, laundry marks and the rifle that had been caught by the top fire escape landing.

Moe's determination to get to Maloney's was now intense. But he had to accompany Steve to the Thirteenth Precinct house where his impatience grew as Steve seemed to tell a lot more than was absolutely necessary. And as a result of Steve's openness, Crawford and Tonto were summoned, and they took up even more time. Most irritating of all was Crawford's inability to remember Moe's answers and asking the same questions over and over again.

"Now what did the man say to you?"

"Aw, come on," Moe protested. "I told you."

"What did you tell me?"

Moe said it again. "He said he didn't want any trouble."

"That's why he was up there with the rifle? After pigeons, maybe?"

"Naw, he was *giving* trouble. He didn't want to take any."

"What trouble was he giving?"

"He took a couple shots at us. Look!" Moe turned his bloody shoulder for inspection.

Steve interrupted. "He probably saved my life, Crawford. At least that's what he thought he was doing."

Crawford shot him an exasperated look. "So now you're a mind reader, eh?"

"It's the truth," Moe said. "I was trying to save my buddy's life."

"This is worse than the Steve and Tonto show," Crawford snarled. "Steve, the time for you to say your line is after I look at you and ask you a question."

"Sorry."

Crawford turned back to Moe. "From the moment you ran through the roof door . . ."

"I saw the guy jumping over to the next building, like I said. And I heard Steve coming up the stairs behind me. I didn't want Steve to get hurt, so I blocked the door to keep him off the roof. Then the guy took a shot at me and turned to run some more. But I got to him and held him by the throat like this." He demonstrated with the air.

"How tight?"

"So he couldn't get away."

"So he couldn't talk?"

"Not that tight."

"Then what did the guy say?"

"He said he didn't want any trouble."

They went around the rosy several times before Moe and Steve were dismissed with the usual cautionary words about not leaving town. As Moe waited impatiently at the door for Steve, Tonto took Steve aside.

"Maybe you're in the clear now, but take it easy."

"In the clear?"

"The perpetrator fits the description of the hotel sniper..."

"And the rifle...?"

"...Fits the shell casing we found."

"So maybe he was the only one out to get me."

"Anyway, we'll have the Royalton desk clerk come look at the remains."

When Steve got outside, Moe rushed him into a cab, and they took off for Twenty-fourth Street. "You know what that guy with the rifle told me?" Moe asked.

"Well, I heard you tell Crawford half a dozen times, didn't I?"

"Hey, you think I'm crazy?"

"What?"

"I didn't tell him everything."

"Why not?"

"They'd've got in the way. You know how cops are."

"Moe, in one sentence, what did the guy tell you?"

"Who hired him."

"In another sentence, who?"

"That bozo Maloney."

"Which Maloney?"

"What do you mean, Steve? There more than one?"

"There are at least two. Which one was it?"

"Gee, I dunno. He just said Maloney."

17

Outside Maloney's building, there were forty or fifty young people wearing blue jeans and sneakers, carrying placards, marching in a long oval line and chanting, "FREEdom! Not FURious!"

The ex-cop doorman had found his way to the center of the oval and was having a one-sided argument with passing protestors. "Come on, we got a lot of old people living here. This kind of thing upsets them. You guys got a beef, fine. That's your right. But take it to City Hall, will you?"

Someone offered him a package shaped like an oversized candy kiss. The doorman refused the gift. "Okay, you want me to get tough about it? I'll call the cops."

The arms offering presents rose as they neared him and fell as they passed, like so many Rockettes' legs at Radio City Music Hall. This confused the doorman for a moment, but then he pushed his way angrily through the chorus line and retreated to the security of his lobby.

Steve and Moe stood on the road side of the parade, and each accepted one of the packages. The blue-bordered wrapping had a message.

FREEdom! Not FURious!

Maloney rhymes with baloney.
But it's no baloney that Harry Maloney
   is wrapped up in FURious furs.
FURious means the senseless slaughter of
   thousands of helpless sables so that
   silly women may affect importance.
Please join us in our fight for life.
Contact FREE (Foundation for Rehabilitation, Education and Enlightenment).

There was a Village address, phone number and an explanation of what was in the package.

This is FREE incense.
Burn it for the cause.
We hope its pleasant aroma will one day
   permeate the city.
And FREE will no longer have to put up
   a stink about atrocities like FURious.

It was a pretty big hunk of incense, and it smelled like Jody's apartment. Then, speak of the devil, there was Jody among the protesters. Steve marched along beside her, and Moe tagged along.

"Jody, how did FREE find out Maloney was connected with FURious?"

"Mr. Smith found out. I don't know how. Does it matter?"

"Yeah, it might. Where is he?"

"Probably at headquarters. Who's your friend?"

Steve introduced Moe who adopted his

aggressive-toward-broads attitude, which made Jody giggle.

As they reached the lobby doors, Steve and Moe spun off the line.

"You!" The doorman recognized Steve.

"Yeah, me."

The doorman nodded toward Moe. "This guy a cop?"

"Just another friend of Harry Maloney."

"Well, where are your cop friends? They coming?"

"They supposed to?"

"Yeah. We can't have this stuff going on in this neighborhood."

"Well, we'll go on up."

"Wait a minute." The doorman picked up the phone and called upstairs, but there was no answer. "He ain't home."

"Maybe he's just drunk."

"All I know is he ain't picking up on the house phone. So what can I tell you?"

"You can tell us to go up and try the bell."

"Not allowed."

"We had to wait for an answer last time. Try again."

Again no answer. But before the doorman could turn back to Steve to tell him so, there was a renewed, louder chanting from the FREE people outside. The doorman rushed out to quiet them down.

Steve took Moe's arm. "Come on."

They got into the elevator and pressed the tenth floor button. The elevator rose to the ninth and stopped. The doors didn't open.

"Awright, awright," the doorman's voice came over the speaker. "Now I'm bringing you two wiseacres right back to where you belong, just as soon as I take care of the other troublemakers outside."

They were stuck for eight minutes. It seemed longer. The least of it was that it got close and hot inside. It was the thought of the space beneath their feet that made Steve start dirty sweating. He could control his vertigo for most elevator rides, but he had trouble in any that got stuck above the third floor. He finally yelled at the intercom, "Come on! Make up your mind! Up or down, but get us out of here!"

Moe put a firm hand on his buddy's shoulder. "Take it easy, Steve."

"Awright," the doorman's voice finally said. "Down it is."

The elevator descended to the lobby. When the doors opened, Crawford and Tonto got in.

"Now you go up," said the doorman.

"He's not supposed to be home," Steve told the detectives as the elevator rose again.

"We'll see," Crawford said.

"What brought you?"

"We just want to see if poor Harry's being disturbed by that awful demonstration."

Tonto was more helpful. "Now that everybody seems to know Maloney's involved with FURious, he might have more to tell us."

Nobody answered the bell at 10-H. Steve had another gut feeling. Crawford had a key. Once inside, they found Harry slumped over in the living room, the same characteristic pose Steve had seen him in two days ago. Even the stereo was still playing classical music. But this time Harry couldn't be revived. And there was no chance he ever would be.

18

Maloney was embalmed with Jack Daniels. A magnum bottle on the coffee table was empty. It looked like he had finally succeeded in drinking himself to death.

"I doubt it," Crawford said.

Moe had been spellbound by the sight, or maybe because his mission had been thwarted. But now he found his voice. "I saw it happen once."

"Get the civilian out," Crawford said.

Tonto took Moe to the door. "Get that arm looked after."

Moe left obediently and Tonto came back. Crawford was crouched awkwardly over the body, listening for any sign of life. Then he stepped back on the balls of his feet. "Yeah, he bought it all right. He's past the fourth stage."

"Drunk dead," Steve observed.

Crawford kept his hands in his pockets to be sure he didn't touch anything. "Blood around the lips," he observed.

"How long ago?" Tonto asked.

"Maybe an hour. Maybe less. That's not our department."

Tonto went down to the car to radio for the usual crew that had to be summoned; homicide or suicide, it was all the same at this point. Steve went down to send the demonstrators home. But the oval line melted together, chanted louder and faster and moved toward a passing cab. The cab sped off toward the east. Steve pulled Jody out of the crowd. "Let's get out of here."

He took her to the White Horse Tavern downtown. It used to be his favorite bar until, as he got older, the clientele seemed to get younger. But still, every once in a while, you'd catch it on a good day when it wasn't crowded and no one was playing the juke box. This happened to be a good day. They sat in a small dark room off the bar. Steve ordered an ale and Jody had a bottle of Perrier Water. He told her about Harry Maloney.

"He drank a lot?" she asked.

"He drank a lot."

"And they think that killed him?"

"Not sure. Maybe I did."

"You?"

"It's beginning to look like half the people I meet lately get killed before I see them again." He caught himself being maudlin and smiled. "Yeah, Jody, booze could've done it. Moe said he saw it happen once."

"It happened here."

"Where?"

"Right there in the White Horse."

"You mean you saw it?"

"No! Steve, don't tell me you didn't know this is where Dylan Thomas used to hang out."

"I guess I did. I never paid much attention to that stuff."

"I think he was sitting right over there." She pointed to a table by the window. "He said something about just having downed a lot of straight whiskeys."

"How many?"

"I think it was thirty-six British measures, or eighteen American. He said he thought that was a record. His last words."

"You'd think he'd have gone unconscious before it killed him."

"Mr. Smith saw it happen, too, once. That's one of the reasons FREE's opposed to drinking." She saw Steve look at his ale. "No offense. Thanks for bringing me here. I needed a place to get peaceful again."

"Yeah, a crowd like that can get ugly."

"Not my crowd. Not FREE people."

"Then what were they going to do to that cab?"

"Just yell at it a little."

"Why?"

"Because the passenger was wearing one of those furs."

Steve's ale mug stopped halfway to his mouth. "What did she look like?"

"I didn't see her face. Just the fur and the blonde hair."

"You sure it was blonde?"

"Yes. Very."

Steve looked at his watch. The incident had happened about an hour ago. By now, Gloria had faded back into hiding.

What to do? The only guy who might've led him to Gloria had just died. If Maloney had been murdered it had probably been by the same assassin who'd been in the apartment on Monday, the ubiquitous cleaning woman. But now that the harridan was a known suspect, how could she get back to Maloney's apartment?

"Did you see anybody strange go into the building while you were demonstrating?"

"What do you mean, strange?"

"Kind of a frowzy woman, white hair, probably wearing some flashy getup."

"No, but I could've missed her."

"She's hard to miss." He gave her the rundown.

"Could she have come up from the basement?" she asked.

"No, the elevator's set to stop at the lobby. She'd have to get in from the outside. How many times did that doorman come out to talk to you guys?"

"Whenever we got especially noisy. Frequently."

So the doorman was frequently diverted from his job. Maybe, then, somebody could get in and out without being seen if the demonstration had been orchestrated properly. This could make FREE an accomplice to murder.

"How did you say you knew Maloney was connected with FURious?"

"Mr. Smith. I don't know how he knew."

"There are guys *in the business*—I heard two of them at the Y—who don't know who's behind FURious. Now don't tell me Mr. Smith is just psychic."

"As a matter of fact, he *is* psychic."

"Enough to pick the right name out of a phone book?"

"Are you making fun of me?"

"Jody, no! Come on, I've never teased you about your enlightenment thing, have I? I don't pretend to understand it, but I respect it. Okay?"

She blushed. "Sorry. You learn to be on the defensive with people who aren't involved themselves."

"But it's obvious, isn't it, that your Mr. Smith has access to privileged information?"

"If you're assuming that he had anything to do with Maloney drinking himself to death, I'd have to say that wasn't worth your time. He's helped people. Right at the meetings, I've seen him turn a drunk or an addict into a person with hope. No sweating it out. No cold turkey. The man's a saint."

"Or a magician."

"Call it what you want. The results are the same."

"I'd still like to look into it."

"Then why don't you take me up on the invitation I made you two months ago?"

"What's that? When did I ever turn down one of your invitations?"

"I invited you to come with me to a FREE meeting. You shied off, so I didn't hound you about it. Your space, my space. But you can still come. There's a meeting tomorrow night."

"You're on."

"Really?"

"Sure."

"The meeting's at eight."

"Pick you up at seven-thirty. What'll I wear?"

"You saw us. Anything you want."

"Blue jeans, sneakers . . ."

"Sure."

"Motif Number Seven."

19

YMCA members were regular in their habits. So if you went there about the same time each day, you'd run into a lot of the same people. It wasn't unusual for Steve to be closeted in the sauna with the same two garment men from four days ago. And it wasn't unusual that they were still on the same topic.

"This, I guarantee, is gonna kill you."

"Such guarantees I can do without."

"I was on my way here, y'see. Now picture this. Ahead of me is a beautiful woman. I mean terrific. Not only is she a knockout, but she is wearing a FURious."

"Surprise, surprise."

"Wait. So I approach this dame. 'Excuse me, miss.' Well, she reels around, and *she* turns out to be a *he*! Yeah, one of them..."

"Transvestites."

"One of them transvestites, I'm telling you. And she...he...*it* is giving me this bitchy look, maybe because I look a little surprised. But I carried it off, it now being easier to be aggressive about my intent."

"About the coat."

"So I said, 'Excuse me, *Miss*.' He begins to look more friendly. So I said it again. 'Excuse me, *Miss*, but I'm in the fur business, and I couldn't help admiring your sable.' He gives me a superior smile and says, 'It's a FURious.' Well, to make a long story short, the guy tells me he got it at one of them thrift shops, the one in midtown."

"Fur-o-rama?" A sneer in the question.

"It was Fur-o-rama."

"I don't get it."

"You don't get it? What else could it be? The FURious thing is going bust. You seen any ads this month?"

"I don't believe it. A sable in a thrift shop?"

"You thought it was gonna be big, right? I knew it would never make it. They overextended themselves with all that fancy promotion and going with such an expensive fur."

"I don't believe it."

"You don't believe it? I'm *telling* you."

Steve was still mulling over the conversation when he got to his building.

"Mr. Hershey!" It was the night man. "Messenger brought this when Herb was on duty."

Steve took the manila envelope from Greenglass Associates and went up to his office. When he got there, he stood before the door a moment, wondering if somebody was waiting for him inside, wondering if someone hadn't gotten the message about the purse being with the police, someone who might think the envelope he held was it.

He drew his gun and burst in, falling into a crouch, the gun in front of him panning left to right.

The place was empty and untouched. He felt safe and foolish.

He locked himself in and sat at the desk where he opened the envelope. Nine eight-by-tens clipped together labeled "March." Seven more labeled "April." There was also a note from Art. "Here is the material you requested, the pictures representing our total magazine campaign to date. The periodical used is indicated on the back of each shot." Steve turned one packet over and saw *Mademoiselle* written on the bottom shot.

The note went on, "The March dates specified for airport saturation are not available at the moment. However, the April dates are as follows: The 12th, 15th, 20th, 23rd, 25th, and one coming up on the 30th. We have, as I believe I indicated to you, received no dates for May or any other month. I trust your ongoing discretion in protecting my anonymity in this matter."

Steve spread the seven April pictures in front of him. Gloria was in three, Ann in four. Their purses looked different in each, except that each had that oval silver plate under the clasp.

Crawford and Tonto would both be off duty now. So Steve put the materials back in the envelope and slept with them under his pillow that night.

Thursday, April 26

He was still alive the next morning. That made him feel good all through his shower. Until his shave. Ideas always came when he was shaving. This morning he wondered if anyone was going to want to keep the pictures from police scrutiny, as they'd wanted to keep the purse.

That bothered him until he dressed (Motif Number Two: brown slacks, corduroy sports jacket, beige shirt, no tie), and then he comforted himself with the thought that the pictures were readily available on any newsstand. Except they weren't this month. Except no one may have thought about putting them together before.

The more he worried, the angrier he got. And the angrier he got, the more he was determined not to worry. He did take the precaution of rolling the pictures into a thin tube, wrapping an elastic around them, and putting them under Bertha's shoulder holster.

Maybe he should have gone directly to the station house to unload the Greenglass stuff. But risky or not, he decided there was someplace else he ought to go first.

20

Fur-o-rama was a small place in a cellar in the East Fifties. The sign outside said, "ANYONE CAN AFFORD BEAUTY! WALK DOWN AND GIVE YOURSELF A LIFT!"

"Something for the little woman?" It was a young man in a plaid sports jacket. He was being very friendly. He was also being watched by an older man at the back of the store.

Steve smiled back. "Well, maybe. My wife's been after me about something called . . . what is it? . . . FURious?"

The man kept smiling. "Oh yes, FURious. It's very popular with the ladies today. We happen to have just one left."

"May I see it?"

"Certainly, sir. Right this way." He led Steve to a rack against the wall and held out a sable sleeve. "You don't see many sables anymore. You don't see many like this one."

"So far I only see the sleeve."

The older man had come up behind them. "I'll

tend to this gentleman, Max. Go check those invoices."

Max retreated in defeat.

"How do you do?" The man shook Steve's hand. "My name's Max. Max, Senior. I see you're interested in our FURious number. It's the last one we have. An excellent value."

"Did you have many?"

"To tell you the truth, we only had two. They're very hard to come by. Ours were brought in by models. Maybe you've seen the ads?"

"No, can't say I have."

"No reason you should, of course. They were all in ladies' magazines. I'm sure your wife saw them."

Max took the coat off the rack and held it out. "About your wife's size, do you think?"

"Looks like it."

"Notice the fullness. Looks like a fifty thousand dollar coat, doesn't it?"

"Fifty thousand!?"

"Let me tell you, this coat would be a steal at forty thousand. Your wife would be able to tell you that."

"Well, how much is it?"

"Twenty thousand, nine hundred, and it's yours."

"Gee, how can you sell it for that?"

"There are lots of reasons. You look like an intelligent young man, so I'm going to be honest with you. We run on a low overhead here. Also, we deal only in previously owned furs, so we're able to buy for less. Finally, to tell you the truth, this coat isn't all it seems to be."

"Your son said it was sable."

"Genuine sable. But there isn't as much real fur in it as it looks. Feel that," he said, exposing the rich gold lining. It felt like a deep quilting underneath. "You see?" Max smiled. "It's all bunched up in there. Now trace the line up and down."

Steve ran his fingers and thumb down the long outline of a section of hidden padding. "Yeah?"

"It is this," Max announced, "that gives the coat its body. It looks like a lot of sable, and the lady feels rich who wears it. But the gentleman who buys it for her doesn't have to go broke making her happy. That's the way everything should be. Am I right or am I wrong?"

"You're right. But twenty thousand is still a lot of money."

"No, wait. I'll show you." Max took small scissors from his vest pocket and aimed them at the stitching on the lining.

Steve protested, "Hey, don't go cutting it apart for me."

"Listen, no trouble. It's nothing to sew back lining. I want you should see this. It's really ingenious." A corner of the lining freed, Max folded it back and exposed some tubes of quilted fabric, each about an inch wide. "Just look at that workmanship. You're not just buying a coat with a respectable amount of sable. You're buying a piece of engineering. Not only does this construction make the coat seem fuller. It also gives it life."

"What do you mean?"

"Picture this. Let's say you have some inflated inner tubes. You old enough to remember them?"

"Definitely."

"So you got these tubes filled with air, right?" Max watched Steve closely, wondering if his analogy was too archaic maybe. "Circles of tubing to go inside car tires, right?"

Steve reassured the older man. "We used to use them when we went swimming."

"You got it. So think of an inner tube, or a life preserver, or whatever. You've got three of them, and you put your arms through them. You follow?"

"I got you."

"Now what happens when you squeeze your arms?"

"I squeeze the air out in front of me."

"So near you the rubber contracts, and away from you it expands. You got an action and you got a reaction, right?"

"Right."

"Now something similar happens with the FURious. Action and reaction. First of all, sable, it's a very light fur so it has life when it moves. In addition, you got this special construction. The wearer's body moves against one side of the coat and the opposite side reacts."

"What do they use for padding?"

"Let's see."

"No, don't go cutting it anymore."

"Don't worry." He exposed a small section at the bottom of a line of quilting. There was a foam material inside.

Steve said, "It must be very warm."

"Well, you don't buy a fur coat to stay cool."

"Very interesting. But, like I said, I want to think about it."

"I'd like to be your furrier."

"Okay, if I decide, you're it."

"This coat won't stay on the floor long. You want to put a deposit, and we'll hold it for you."

"No, I want to think about it."

"I figured you was interested."

"I am. But I'm shopping around."

"I can't make the price any lower."

"No, the price is fine."

"I figured you was interested. That's why I hacked it up to show you."

Pressure.

"I'll be in touch," Steve said, turned abruptly and left the store.

21

"Trying to reach you all morning," Tonto said. "Jonathan Maloney's on his way, and you're just in time to sit in."

"Why would I be in on it, as far as Jonathan's concerned?"

"You're a guy who saw the deceased brother near the end..."

"... And I've come along to offer my helpful information..."

"... But you don't know very much..."

"... And I don't want to be involved because I've been shot at."

"And, if it'll help," Tonto grinned, "I'll suggest you're next to useless as far as we're concerned."

"While our little drama's going on, maybe you can get somebody working on this." Steve turned over the Greenglass stuff. "Get a good magnification on the silver plates on the purses in the April ads. See if they're all the same as the one we've got. You did get . . . ?"

"Came today."

Jonathan Maloney was in the interrogation room with Crawford when Tonto brought Steve in.

Besides being alive, Jonathan was in other ways the direct opposite of his late brother, as Greenglass' description had already suggested. He cut a good figure—trim in a dark business suit. And he was exceptionally alert, with invisible antennae reaching out for information—actual or implied. His eyes darted about a lot, and there was a twitch in the corner of the left one, the outward manifestation of the wheels turning inside his head. He was, in other words, the kind of guy you'd want to be careful with.

"This is Steve Hershey," Tonto introduced him. "He's a private detective."

Crawford said, "Steve's involved with the case and saw your brother three days ago. We thought he might help us throw some light on what happened."

Steve shook Jonathan's hand. "I'm not really *involved* with the case. If I can help about your brother, fine. But that's the end of it."

Jonathan had a firm grip. His eyes dug into Steve before he nodded and sat.

Crawford remained standing. "I've been filling Mr. Maloney in on what we know. I think he understands that we're here to assure ourselves his brother died without any help so we can close the book."

Jonathan nodded. Crawford sat. Jonathan looked at Steve.

Steve took the cue. "I was working on something for one of my clients. I have to keep the details confidential, of course. But it led me to your brother's place, and he was drunk when I got there. I've told these detectives that your brother seemed to be a confirmed alcoholic and that's probably what killed him."

Jonathan looked to Crawford.

"Yeah," Crawford said. "And we don't have any reason to doubt it. If we'd thought your brother had anything to do with the Brewer murder, we'd have taken him into custody. Too bad for him we didn't. But that's just Monday morning quarterbacking right now. What can you tell us about him, Mr. Maloney?"

Jonathan looked sad. When he spoke, his voice was smooth and well-modulated, like it had been trained. "What can one man say about his brother? What can another man want to know at a time like this?"

It didn't go over anyone's head that he answered a question with questions. Crawford asked another. "Do you have any reason to suspect someone'd want to kill him?"

"Kill Harry? Why bother? He was killing himself as fast as he could, and now he's completed the job."

"Then you believe your brother did in fact drink himself to death."

"How else? He was a hopeless alcoholic, a sadness to our parents, rest their souls, and the reason they wanted to leave this earth. Of course it was suicide. Intentional or not, I don't know. Subconsciously, it must have been intentional. Very much like something that happened when I was in the Army. My unit was on a train, on the first leg of a journey to Vietnam. Hardly any of us wanted to go. One young man opened his gullet and poured a fifth of whisky down, then fell over dead. Perhaps my brother had more tolerance than that soldier, but one cannot resist forever. Were there any signs of violence?"

"Not really," Tonto said. "A little blood on the

gums and lips. He could have done that himself."

"I found him like that once," Jonathan said. "It was as though he could not shove the glass against his mouth fast enough. He drank with desperation, with an unhappiness I have never understood."

Crawford scratched his chin. "Ever try to make him stop?"

"You do what you can. But when a man gets to be forty-five, it is often too late. Recently, I tried to give him a sense of worth by giving him a job, but this final attempt to save him was apparently as unsuccessful as the others."

"What kind of a job?"

"Oh, nothing important, only some trifling assignment I thought he could handle."

"And did he?"

"I don't like to speak ill of the dead. But if the business succeeds, it will not be because of any contributions made by my brother." Jonathan turned to Steve. "I imagine you saw him at his worst. Did he strike you as a competent businessman?"

"Afraid not."

"He rambled in his speech, did he not?"

"Definitely."

"Giving out details to strangers like yourself, yes?"

"Yes," Steve lied, then saw the wheels behind Jonathan's eyes go into high gear.

"But were you able to understand what he was talking about?"

"Some babbling about furs or something. I wasn't interested and didn't pay much attention."

Jonathan looked helpless. "You see? We had a campaign based on careful strategy, and secrecy was an important part of that. But my brother mentions it to you. I was a fool to get him involved."

"Well, the only real damage he did was to himself."

"Yes. Yes." Jonathan looked to Crawford. "I must make arrangements. When can you release the body?"

"Soon. Soon. If you'll leave your address and phone, we'll be in touch."

Jonathan gave them both.

Crawford wrote them down. "If you're away, will there be anyone there to get our call?"

"I am a bachelor."

Steve asked, "Do you need me anymore?"

"No, you can go. You can both go. Thanks very much for your cooperation, Mr. Maloney." Crawford had trouble sounding sincere.

"Can I use a phone?" Steve asked.

"Use the one outside."

Steve rushed out of the room and wrote down Jonathan's address and phone number before he forgot them. He called Jody to confirm their date for the evening. He was hanging up when Crawford and Tonto appeared.

"He's gone," Tonto said. "In a big, shiny limo."

"I'm beginning to get the feeling," Steve said, "that everybody knows at least one story about someone who drank himself to death. Moe does. My girlfriend does."

"Is that all you got out of our little chat?" Crawford asked.

"Sure. He didn't want to tell us anything. He came here to find out what we knew."

"So," Crawford shook his head, "it was a standoff." Tonto took a drawing from his desk and handed it to Steve. "How about it? That your girlfriend?"

Steve looked at a good facsimile of the cleaning

woman. "That's her all right. The other guy she worked for . . .?"

"Thursh. He says this looks like her."

"You got it circulated?" Steve asked.

"No," Crawford said. "We just got it made up to use for toilet paper."

"Still," Tonto said, "it stretches the imagination to believe someone who looks like that got in and out of your building without being seen."

"Can I keep this one?" Steve asked.

"Be my guest."

A call came from the lab. Then they went to a small room where a young man with glasses was putting slides in a tray. "Good timing," he said. He set the tray on the projector. "We've just got the April ads so far, but those were the ones you put the rush on. Okay, we blew up the areas of the photographs where the purses were and, even though we lost a generation in the process, the results are interesting." He turned off the lights, flipped on the projector and focused the first slide on the screen. "This is the plate on the purse you sent us today." New slide. "And this is the purse in one of the pictures we got today."

"They're the same," Steve said.

"Another shot."

"Still the same."

"Precisely. The purse we have matches two of the pictures. But you can tell by the wristwatches that two different girls hold each purse. What does that etching look like to you?"

"A design of some kind," Crawford guessed.

"Initials," Tonto said. "A Q and an O."

"It also looked like a number to me," Steve said. "A 20."

"Very good," said the projectionist. "Now hold that thought while we see the third slide."

New slide. "It's changed, hasn't it?"

"A 12," Steve said.

"Precisely. Moving right along..." He flipped four more slides. "A 15, a 23, a 25 and a 30."

Tonto summarized. "Two 20s, a 12, a 15, a 23, a 25 and a 30."

"Precisely."

"Precisely!" Crawford barked. "Precisely *what*?"

"I'll tell you precisely what," Steve said. "Those are the April dates when Greenglass was told to have models at the airport."

22

The meeting was in a basement room that the church made available to spiritual and semi-spiritual groups dedicated to doing good works. Mostly young people sat on the floor surrounding a platform. For the older, the stiffer, the less enlightened or the timid there were a few rows of folding chairs around the perimeter.

Steve, dressed in Motif Number Seven, sat in the back row of chairs. Jody, who had forgone her usual spot on the floor to sit beside him, held his hand and tried to control her nervousness about his being there.

"Try lowering your critical vibrations," she told him.

"My what?"

"Suspend your disbelief until it's over."

"Jody," he protested, "I'm completely neutral so far."

"No, you're looking for something. If you don't turn that off, you'll miss what's really here."

"Turn it off? How?"

"Just make your mind a blank."

"That's easy for you to say."

Steve did his best to think of nothing, found that nothing was just another kind of something, then gave up and concentrated on the pre-meeting activity around him.

Warm, open smiles flashed all around. People were hugging each other as casually as Steve might shake hands. Some sat cross-legged, eyes lidded, motionless, breathing deeply the incense-laden air. One girl, in sharp contrast, seemed to be in pain and was rocking back and forth. She was interrupted by many, received their hugs, their smiles, their kisses, then resumed her rocking. Steve thought she looked like a junkie.

A young man with light-brown hair that hung just below the top of his madras shirt collar circulated among the floor sitters, greeting each one, stopping to chat with some. Steve saw Jody's eyes following the man and, noticing that the guy was more or less on the handsome side, began to give off more critical vibrations.

A stir in the room. It swept from the back to the front, gaining in intensity as it moved, and all heads—except the rocking girl's—turned to the door.

No one had heard him enter, but he stood there now, looking around, beaming. He wore white duck pants, a white dress shirt (three buttons open) and a silver medallion. He was well-built, black-haired. He could have been middle-aged or younger; it was hard to tell, probably because of prominent bone structure in the face and eyes that shone with perception and confidence.

His head turned to the left, and his eyes fell on Steve. He smiled broadly and sidled between the rows of chairs toward him. "Welcome," he whispered and held out both his hands like he was expecting to be hugged. Steve held out one of his, and the man clasped it from both sides with a strong grip. "Welcome!" he repeated. "I'm Mr. Smith."

"Steve Hershey." He wouldn't want to admit it to Jody, but he could feel great strength in Smith. If he knew a man was physically strong, Steve tended to have all kinds of confidence in him, an attitude that remained deep-seated despite recent experiences with Moe. It was more than strength in Smith, though. It was power, too. He was Spencer Tracy and Burt Lancaster all rolled into one. Maybe that's why he seemed like an old friend.

Smith turned to the others and held up Steve's hand. "My friends, this is Steve."

"Welcome!" they chanted in unison.

"Steve..." Smith began, then paused, his eyes closed, "...is a student of mankind. Steve knows people. He is an... investigator of people. In a sense, we are all investigators of life, and Steve belongs among us. Once more, please..."

"Welcome, Steve," the crowd chanted.

Steve nodded foolishly, and his hand was returned to him. It smelled of incense.

Smith moved gracefully through the crowd, touching random shoulders as he went. "There is no pressure on Steve."

Steve's jaw dropped. He whispered to Jody, "Did you tell him I was coming? That I was a private investigator? How I felt about pressure?"

"No, of course not," Jody whispered back. "Shhh."

"No pressure," Smith was saying, "on any of you to testify at this meeting. Some of you have never spoken to reveal your hearts. It is not necessary. You speak by just being here. Welcome all."

Smith reached the platform, turned and smiled at the audience, then went into a hushed conference with the somewhat handsome man in the madras shirt.

Steve whispered, "Are you sure?"

"You just don't understand, do you?"

"I'm trying to."

"Some people are just sensitive to other people. He sensed who you are."

Smith sat in a chair on the platform while the good-looking man stood on the edge and made some announcements, referring to slips of paper in his hand. "A car is leaving on Saturday for Boston. Room for two. Anyone interested?"

Jody had been thinking. "Steve, Mr. Smith is a very exceptional man. If you weren't so negative, you'd have known that the minute you saw him. How do you think he gets all these people to come here every week?"

"Tell me."

"People are just naturally attracted to a man like that. A good man. I hear he's an ordained minister . . . and a guru. He doesn't say so himself, but he carries it with him, and people know. If a few people know, it gets around. There are twice as many here tonight as there were a month ago."

Steve patted her arm, and she pulled it away. "I'm sorry," he said.

"Just don't be patronizing, all right?"

"Sure. All right. I'm not *totally* insensitive, Jody."

"Then will you just be here, and just see what happens?" Her attention riveted on the front of the room.

All of the announcements made, Smith came to the front of the platform and put his arm around the young man. "Thank you, Brian."

Brian nodded and joined the others on the floor.

"I look at you, and you look back at me," Smith said. "But I see in your faces something that shouldn't be there."

The crowd hung on every word.

"I see adoration. I don't want that. Never forget my name is Mr. Smith, not the name I was born with, but the one I chose. Mr. Smith! An alias. A non-descriptive label. I am just another person." He gestured to his chair. "And that is not a throne. If you idolize me, you put yourselves outside what FREE is all about. Look inside yourselves and you will find much more to worship there."

But Smith seemed to be getting the opposite effect he intended. The more he protested his ordinariness and the more sincerely humble he got, the more saintly he appeared.

"It is only finding the best inside ourselves, not in leaders, that we can truly contribute to the best in others. Do you accept this?"

A feeble response, "Yes."

Smith raised his voice. "Do you *believe* it?!"

"Yes!" More conviction this time.

"*Do you believe it*?!"

"*Yes!*"

"*Say it!*"

"*We believe it!*"

"Good. Now let's each take a moment. Close your eyes. Don't look at me. Don't think about me. Look inside yourself. And perhaps Bruce will play something for us."

A bearded young black man sat on the edge of the platform and began to strum a guitar. All eyes closed, except Steve's, and the lines drained from the faces, as Bruce sang:

> FREE is me
> and what I've got to be.
> Only if I'm flying high
> Can I show my brother freedom,
> de dum de dum.
> Freedom, de dum de dum.
> Only flying sep'rately
> can we be together FREE.

The guitar continued, as Smith spoke softly. "You are the leader of yourself. You are the follower of your destiny." Pause. "All right. Eyes open. Thank you, Bruce. That was very nice."

The guitar stopped.

"There is someone here tonight who isn't free yet. She is in great pain. And I believe tonight we can help her. Because I believe she will accept our help. Let's see, shall we?"

Smith nodded to Bruce who began to play the song again. Then he led the others in singing it. They sang it seven times and, as they were beginning the eighth, the girl Steve thought was a junkie got slowly to her feet and stepped onto the platform. Smith put his arm around her shoulders as they finished the song. Then there was silence and waiting.

"I am a drug addict," the girl said in a spaced-out monotone, reading the words off a celestial teleprompter. "I don't want to be this way. That's why I've been coming to these meetings. I haven't had a fix today, and I don't want to have one tomorrow. I think I've found the strength to stop. I still have this." She took a small cellophane packet from her knitted shoulder bag and held it up. "This is heroin. I had to sell my body to buy it. I thought, well, after this, *then* I'll kick the habit. But something caught up with me and stopped me, something I was getting at these meetings. Now I want to get rid of this bag. I want to give it to you,

Mr. Smith, and I want you to get rid of it for me."

The crowd cheered as Smith took the packet and held it up. "Does anyone here want this?" Smith asked.

"No!"

"Are you sure?"

"Yes!"

"Yes what?"

"Yes, we're sure!"

"Good." He turned to the girl. "Do you want to share your name with us? You don't have to."

"Susan," she said. "Sue."

Smith spoke to the others. "We must commend Sue's courage. It was not easy for her to carry this without using it. But, my friends, we have only won a skirmish, not the whole battle." He turned to Sue. "I want you to sit in my chair tonight. And I want you to hold this on your lap."

She looked away. "I don't want to see it again."

"Yes, my dear, but the reason? You don't want to see it again because you are still tempted, and we must rip out that temptation for good. So sit here and work on it. And try to feel the love that we're all projecting to help you."

Sue reluctantly took the packet and sat in the chair.

"Our friend Sue knows," Smith told the crowd, "that she can take the heroin orally and that will ease her pain. If she chooses to do that, we won't stop her. We won't love her any less. But tonight, if she can, she must sit with the temptation on her lap and conquer it."

Steve looked at Jody. "That's crazy."

Jody's attention was on the platform, and it took a moment for Steve's comment to register. "What?"

"He's taking a hell of a chance."

"He always takes chances. That's how he

works."

"If there was a cop here . . ."

"Shhh."

Sue was slightly doubled over in the chair. Smith lightly rubbed the top of her head. "We believe in you," he said. "We expect nothing of you. Whatever you do, you must do. Whatever you do, we will love you. But we will share your joy if you let the temptation go."

"Bullshit!" Steve hissed, but Jody didn't hear him.

Smith stepped to the front of the platform. "My friends, what do we say?"

"An addict has had it!"

"Again."

"An addict has had it!"

"Yes, an addict has had it. We know addiction is partly in the mind. We know that too often the body addiction is conquered and the psychological addiction is not. That's why addicts remain addicts. Tonight, Sue is attempting to root the addiction out of her mind. If she does, she will be cured." He hung his head a moment. "We must be honest with ourselves. Our work with addicts has not been as successful as it should be. But we are not defeated. We will win each battle until we win the war. Let's have a report."

A girl stood near the front. "Well, the addict troops have made a little progress, I guess. More people are accepting the incense and, if they do, maybe they'll do like we say on the wrappers, breathe FREE incense into their bodies and keep the junk out." She sat back down.

"Some encouragement," Smith said. "Perhaps now we are turning the corner and there will be new, healthy life all over. Life for the addicts. Life for the alcoholics. Life for the fur-bearing animals. Let's have a success story now. Let's see if we can encourage Sue to become a former addict."

A number of hands shot up.

"Oh, just seeing all those brown and white doves waving in the air is encouragement. Keep those hands up high." He went to the back of the chair and told Sue, "Look up." She did, and he pointed out to the audience. "You see all those hands? Each one of them belongs to someone who has conquered a problem at least as bad as yours seems to you now. Or to someone who has helped another conquer such a problem." He clapped his hands together. "I know! Let's hear Brian's story!"

Applause. Brian stood. "Well, most of you have heard it. But I used to be one of those guys slugging down cheap wine in doorways, panhandling for what it cost. Then I tried putting the touch on Mr. Smith, and he promised me a whole case of wine if I came to one FREE meeting. Well, I came to the meeting, and I never did get that wine."

Laughter.

"We are all proud of Brian," Smith said. "What do we say, Brian?"

Brian raised a fist in the air and shouted, "A boozer's a loser!"

"Everybody!" Smith shouted, pointing to Brian.

"A boozer's a loser!"

He pointed at Sue. "And what else?"

"An addict has had it!"

"Are we FREE?"

"Yes!"

"I can't hear you!"

"*Yes!*"

"Good. Ah, my friends, it is not true what most people think, that alcohol is not dangerous. Most of you have heard the story before. But for the benefit of Steve back there and any other newcomers, let me tell it again. It was during the Vietnam war. After basic training. And I was on a troop train that was filled with despair. Men around me were drinking heavily, and I confess I was one of them. On a dare, one of the boys in my outfit..." He paused. His face changed, transformed into a mask of unhappiness. Smith suddenly became the young soldier of his story. No one stirred, everyone caught up in the drama. "This boy..." Smith lifted an imaginary bottle. "This boy raised a full fifth of rotgut and drank it down." Smith became himself again. "My friends, that man died right on the spot!"

Jody turned to Steve. "See?"

"Huh?"

"Remember I told you about that?"

Steve nodded absently, preoccupied with the similarity to Jonathan Maloney's story. He thought about it through most of the rest of the meeting, only vaguely aware that there were other testimonials, more singing, more catch phrases from Smith echoed by the others. He brought his full attention back to the meeting when he heard Smith mention the group's campaign against FURious. Then Steve raised his hand.

Smith pointed to him. "Yes, Steve? Question?"

"Yes sir. I'd like to know..."

"Stand up, Steve."

"I *am* standing up."

"Oh, sorry. Go on."

"I'm very interested in this FURious thing, myself. In fact, that's why I came. I think I'd like to join you."

"You'd be most welcome to join the FURious troops, or the addict troops or the boozer troops or all three, Steve."

"Yeah, well, FURious to start with. I saw your demonstration outside Harry Maloney's apartment building. But now I hear Maloney's dead. In fact, he died from drinking, just like you said."

"You see?" Smith asked the others. "You see how things begin to add up? It's almost like a play, isn't it?"

"Yes, it is." Steve regained the floor. "But if I join the FURious troops, what are we going to do next?"

"Continue our protests wherever they'll do the most good."

"Yeah, but now that Maloney's dead, where do we go? Do we know who else is behind it?"

Smith smiled. "The marching orders will be forthcoming."

"When? Are we going to find out tonight?"

Smith was exceptionally alert now and seemed to be enjoying the interchange, like a comic who could get laughs with hecklers. "Tonight? No, Steve, not tonight."

"Okay, I'll buy that. But can we at least find out how we knew that Harry Maloney was one of the people behind it?"

"I will reveal that at the proper time."

"This time isn't proper?"

Smith smiled like he was sharing a private joke with the others. He glanced back at the junkie who was rocking on the chair, the packet still on her lap, then back at Steve.

"Steve," Smith said, "you are new here, and you don't yet understand the importance of the trust we have in each other. It's all tied up with each person's space and the right to be free in that space. We hardly ever ask direct questions like yours. You see, direct questions only threaten our freedom. We give information freely when we freely choose. I can't let you have a a part of my freedom by answering your question, at least not as directly as you ask it. But I will tell you that I have my sources, and those sources must remain confidential for now. Will you accept that?"

Steve figured Smith had won another skirmish, and he sat back down.

After Smith saw Steve's head sink from his line of vision, he asked the troops, "Will you *all* accept that?"

"Yes!"

"Do you believe it?"

"Yes!"

"Yes what?"

"We believe it!"

"Good." Smith looked back at Sue, then to the audience with a nod. "I think it's happened." He went to the side of the platform where someone sat by a table filled with incense packets. He took a packet and returned to Sue. "Will you give me your package now in exchange for mine?" he asked her.

She looked up and nodded. By this time, she looked more peaceful and without pain. She stood and handed the heroin to Smith, exchanging it for the incense. Everyone applauded wildly. Smith put his arm around Sue, and they all sang another chorus of the FREE song.

"Join your friends, my friend," he told her.

Smiling, she descended to the hugs of those nearest her.

Smith held the heroin in the air. "Who wants to go to the toilet?"

Laughter and several volunteers. He honored one of them who left, returning a moment later without the heroin.

"Now, my friends, I have an announcement," Smith said. "It is this: I must leave you soon."

Some gasped.

"Yes, I must. My work here is about to end for me. I have succeeded in making myself unnecessary, and it is time for me to go on to something new. It will happen to each of you one day, too, as you continue to grow in freedom. It is an essential part of the process we are all involved in. And now, if I may be permitted the choice of a successor to lead these meetings..."

He held out his hand to Brian who joined him on the platform. "Brian will conduct the next meeting under my guidance. And the week after that he will be on his own. Let's give our Brian a vote of confidence."

Applause.

"Thank you. Thank you for allowing me to remain free. Oh, you haven't seen the last of me. I will always be here in spirit. And whenever I'm in town on a Thursday, I'll send my body around, too. You know there will always be a big place in my heart for the fine work that's being done here."

A few people were crying. Jody was one of them. But no one presumed to question the inevitable or impose on Smith's freedom.

"Well, enough of all that," Smith said. "I'll say my goodbyes next time. For now, let us continue as we have done. Come up and get your incense and, until we meet next week, distribute our little packages with love."

The guitar played. People started moving toward the incense table. Jody remained seated, and she didn't bother to dry her eyes until Steve asked her, "Shall we go?"

"In a minute. Come with me first." She led Steve to the front where they waited for her incense.

Smith came up to Steve and clasped him warmly on the shoulder. "Have you enjoyed your first FREE meeting, Steve?"

"It was very enlightening."

"That's the name of the game, Steve. Not

quite as enlightening as you'd hoped, though."
There was a twinkle in his eye.

"Not quite, no."

"Will I see you here next week?"

"I guess I have to keep in touch if I'm going to find out what the FURious troops are going to do next."

Smith smiled. "Welcome." Then he turned and talked to a girl who was crying.

"No collection?" Steve asked Jody. "Last time I was in church, they took up a collection."

Jody smiled, feeling better. "No, Steve, we don't do that."

"What supports the group? There must be expenses. Postage and stuff."

"Some people make donations when they get incense. But it's not required. It's not even encouraged. Mr. Smith says we're supported by our faith."

"Here we go, Jody." The man behind the table gave her a handful of packets. She thanked him and put them in her purse. As an afterthought, she reached over to the table and helped herself to another. When the man saw this, he seemed surprised and instinctively reached out for the packet.

"It's okay," Jody told him. "I've got a partner now. We're burning for two."

The man looked at Smith who gave him a reproving look back.

"Yeah, okay, Jody." The man busied himself looking over the supply he had left before he distributed any more.

Steve was thinking about Smith leaving town, and again about the story of the man who died from drinking whisky.

23

Friday, April 27

This case had brought Steve close to the kind of total involvement Jody claimed was possible through yoga training.

Crawford and Tonto shared Steve's obsession. And now word had come down that the case should be front-loaded, which meant giving it expeditious treatment. Before this elevated status became official, though, they had to meet with the sergeant. Steve, too.

Sergeant Vitale was a stocky man with big black eyebrows that nearly met at the bridge of his once-broken nose. It gave him a distrustful look. He sat behind his desk that had been cluttered in exactly the same way for the past two years, making him look much too busy to bother with trifles.

"Men," he said to Crawford and Tonto, "you know what this is about. We've got two deaths that look connected, and that could mean there are more on the way. Once the media gets wind of it, maybe turns it into serial murders or something, we've got three strikes against us. So we want to nip this in the bud, correct?" He had the irritating quality of waiting for responses to rhetorical questions. Crawford and Tonto nodded, then Vitale went on. "Correct. All right, men, what've we got?" After Crawford reviewed the case, Vitale asked, "That all?"

A "sir" was called for, and Crawford who was over-qualified for Vitale's job let Tonto speak the refrain, "Yes sir."

"You say the cleaning lady apparently carried two laundry sacks from Harry Maloney's apartment the day Ann Brewer died, and the second probably contained Brewer's body. What about the first?"

"The murder weapon," Tonto said. "The fur coat she was smothered with, probably going to a different location."

"And the cleaning lady hasn't been seen since Monday?"

"No sir. We've circulated the sketch of her, but no results so far."

Vitale cocked his head toward Steve without looking at him. "We have only this eyewitness to testify Ann Brewer was actually dead in Harry Maloney's apartment?"

"Yes sir."

"We don't know for sure if Maloney was actually murdered?"

"No sir. But judging by the blood around his mouth, we believe he was forced to drink himself to death."

"And if he was murdered, we don't know how the murderer got in or out."

"No sir. Not exactly."

"What does that mean?"

"Well, the demonstration outside . . ."

"What about it?"

Steve spoke. "It could have been a diversionary action."

Vitale asked Tonto, "Diversionary action?"

"Yes," Tonto said.

"If I might say a word?" Steve asked. Vitale waited. Steve said, "Diversionary action, yes. If it was orchestrated properly, the murderer could have gotten in and out without being noticed, except by the demonstrators who were doing the orchestrating."

Vitale looked at the ceiling. "Possible. But far-fetched."

"Maybe not. I went to a FREE meeting last night, and the guy in charge—calls himself Mr. Smith—told a story about being in the Army and seeing someone drink himself to death. A few hours before that, Harry Maloney's brother told almost the identical story. Now is that a coincidence? Or is it far-fetched to think it wasn't?"

"A connection between Jonathan Maloney and this Mr. Smith?"

"An Army connection."

"Do we have Smith's real name?"

"No sir," Tonto said.

"Maybe we should get it."

"Yes sir."

"Then we might check on his military records, along with Jonathan Maloney's, to see if there is a connection there."

"Yes sir."

"There's another thing," Steve said.

"Yes?"

"If that was a diversionary action outside Harry Maloney's building, this whole FURious thing could be one, too."

Vitale moved a stack of papers on his desk so he could get a better look at Steve. "What've we learned from the advertisements?"

"They were identical except for two things," Steve said. "One the substitution of Ann Brewer or Gloria Emery, the other the purses they held. Each purse had a silver plate with a number etched on it."

"What are the numbers?"

Tonto read from some notes. "The ones for April, a 12, a 15, two 20s, a 23, a 25 and a 30."

Steve said, "The April dates when models were scheduled to be at Kennedy. Including the 23rd when Ann Brewer was murdered."

"Including..." Vitale referred to his desk calendar, "the 30th, this coming Monday. Maybe we should have some men out there to see if the models are diverting us from something."

"Yes sir," Tonto said.

"Probably it isn't a coincidence that the two girls who changed in the ads aren't walking around today. Any idea where this Gloria Emery might be hiding?"

"No sir."

"Well then, gentlemen, we have a lot of opportunities, don't we? A great deal to find out, correct?"

"Yes sir."

"Now there's just one other thing before you embark on this great adventure, and it has to do with this gentleman." He glanced at Steve, then back to Crawford and Tonto. "It's clear that Mr. Hershey may be an invaluable witness in court after we've got this case buttoned up. Now, we like to protest our witnesses, correct?" Pause for a nod from Tonto. "And you tell me Mr. Hershey has been shot at. Twice. Correct?" Pause, nod. "What's being done to protect him, gentlemen?"

Silence.

Steve spoke. "I've requested no protection because I thought it would hamper my movements."

"Officially, I recommend around-the-clock protection for Mr. Hershey. You'll get a memo from me to that effect."

"Yes sir," Tonto said.

"As to his being 'hampered,' as he calls it, the word suggests that he is operating independently as an investigator in a police matter. I officially recommend that he back away from any active participation in this case. Is my official position clear?"

"Yes sir."

Vitale smiled for the first time, the smile looking out of place on his type of face. "Now, off the record, Mr. Hershey, we have a favorite expression around here. 'Cover your ass.' When I write a memo—as I'm going to do—with my official recommendations, that's called 'covering my ass with paper.' It puts the responsibility on whoever wants to accept it if there is any divergence from my recommendations. Whatever you all choose to do, I hope you won't forget to cover your own asses."

Outside the sergeant's office, Steve telephoned his service, and Tonto asked Crawford, "What do you say?"

"I say that sonofabitch must be up for promotion. He's turning into a frigging bureaucrat."

"So what do you say? You've got more at stake than I have."

"We got to take the official recommendation, right? We've got to see Steve's safe. If we're not with him, someone else has to be."

Steve had received a message that Jody called. He called her back. "Jody, what's up?" He listened. "Okay, don't touch anything. I'll be right there." He hung up and turned to the detectives.

"It's out of your territory," he said, "but you might want to come along. I've got a gut feeling about it."

"Oh shit!" Crawford said.

"What is it?" Tonto asked.

"My girl friend, the one who took me to the FREE meeting...?"

"Yeah?"

"Somebody busted into her apartment."

"What'd they take?"

"She's not sure yet. The TV..."

"Anything else?"

"Well, let's go find out."

"Was there something else?" Crawford demanded.

"Let's just go up there."

"Steve!"

"All right... yeah... she thinks they took some incense."

24

They had alerted the Twentieth Precinct to be on the lookout for a television set that had "Off Limits!!" written on it in lipstick, and that this might be no ordinary burglary. And when they arrived at the scene, Crawford and Tonto hid their real interest behind professional detachment.

Steve couldn't be detached. His relationship to the apartment had become so intimate it was synonymous with the relationship he had with Jody. He felt profound outrage, as though she had been raped. The door had been forced open. Drawers had been pulled out and turned over. The sleep sofa was yanked away from the wall, its pillows thrown around the room, one of them slashed and its foam stuffing scattered. There seemed to be nothing untouched.

"This is the way I found it when I came in," she told them. "They didn't take the typewriter or the checkbook or anything else I know of."

Crawford asked, "What would they want with incense?"

Jody had no idea.

The phone rang. Jody answered, then handed the receiver to Crawford. A couple of blocks away a squad car had picked up a suspect carrying a portable television set that looked like Jody's.

They left Jody with instructions to admit the lab man if he arrived, and they drove to the local precinct house five blocks away to take a look at the suspect.

The television set was on the desk of a detective who was typing up a form. The detective was harried and considered the whole thing a big magilla over nothing. But he was cooperating with an urgent request.

Two patrolmen stood nearby.

The suspect who sat by the desk was an ancient, white-haired lady with a tight-lipped, angry look on her face and two weathered shopping bags on the floor beside her.

"A shopping bag lady?" Tonto asked himself.

"Is that the set?" the detective asked in a bored voice.

Steve said it was.

The lady was muttering something.

"What's that?" the detective asked her.

"Talk about police brutality!" she yelled so the whole room could hear her. "You guys want a TV, you get paid enough to buy your own!"

The detective turned to Crawford. "She says she found it in an alley off West End, two blocks north of the scene."

One of the patrolmen said, "When we apprehended her, she was two blocks south and heading south."

"Did she find anything else?" Steve asked.

"No, I didn't!" she said. "There was a lot of crap in that alley. Almost as much as you got in this room."

The detective smiled wearily. "You want me to

book this dangerous character?"

Crawford asked, "Can you turn her over to our custody?"

The detective ripped the form out of the typewriter. "With a hell of a lot of pleasure."

As they were leaving the station, Crawford took a courtly interest in the lady. "You see, ma'am, that TV is stolen property. I apologize for any inconvenience it's caused you, but it's important that we catch the person who took it."

Not wanting to give the impression she was easy, the lady resisted blandishments for five minutes. "Well, the streets aren't safe, for sure. Nobody's out there more than me, and I ought to know."

"Then you'll help us?"

"Will I get my TV back?"

"I told you..." an edge began to creep into Crawford's voice.

"You can have the set," Steve said, "as soon as the police are finished with it."

"Is it working?"

"Definitely."

She took them to an alley and showed them where the set had been, behind some garbage cans. The men searched the alley thoroughly, even sifting through some of the garbage. Then they dismissed the lady and went back to Jody's apartment.

The apartment looked worse with fingerprint powder dusted about. Jody was close to tears. "Look!" she pointed at the room.

"We had to check it out," Crawford apologized.

"Can I clean up this mess now?" she asked. "I can't stand it like this."

The three men went into the hallway to escape the flurry of activity that followed the okay.

"What do you think?" Crawford asked Tonto.

"I think they took the TV two blocks away,

dumped it, then hopped on the subway at Eighty-sixth."

"So," Steve said, "they didn't want the TV after all."

"They'd've been spotted carrying it," Crawford said, "just like that shopping bag lady was."

"They only took it to make it look like a respectable burglary."

"Yeah," Crawford said. "So it was the incense. What was it, the stick stuff?"

"No. The kind that comes in cones." Steve remembered the look that had passed between Smith and the guy distributing incense at the FREE meeting. He knew Jody had taken something meant for someone else. And he knew who knew what.

"Why?" Crawford repeated.

"Beats me," Steve said.

"Okay, we might as well go."

"I'll stay and help Jody," Steve said.

"The only problem with that is every time you go solo, another body turns up."

Tonto supported his partner. "Steve, you kind of owe it to the City of New York to stay with us and keep the population stable. I know how you feel about this . . ."

"You're a clever Indian, but you don't know how I feel about this."

"The thing is," Crawford said, "we don't know yet if it's safe for you on the streets."

"I can take care of myself." Steve said, even though he knew it made him sound like the girl in the monster movie."

Crawford reminded Steve, "You are not Sam Spade."

"Vitale's put the fear of God into you guys, right? If anything happens to me, something happens to you. Tonto could wind up back in uniform. Crawford's pension might turn into a fairy tale. I get it, and I'm sorry about it, but it doesn't change anything."

Crawford's jaw tightened. "I think we could finagle you into protective custody. That the way you want it?"

"Damn it! Goddamn it, Crawford!"

"Easy! We don't need divine assistance to help us screw things up. Answer the question. You want to be locked up or not?"

"Not!"

"Then I'm ordering you to stay here until we get a guy to cover you."

Steve tromped back into the apartment and sank onto the sofa. Jody's vacuum cleaner came into contact with his feet.

"Will you get out of here so I can clean?"

"House arrest," he told her.

Tonto smiled a little and put in a phone call, then left with Crawford. Steve sat sullenly quiet after they'd gone. The vacuum cleaner went off, and then he could hear Jody crying. He pulled her onto the sofa and put his arm around her.

"I just feel so vulnerable now," she said.

"You didn't unwrap any of the incense, did you?"

"No."

"Then don't worry. They got what they were after, and they won't be back. But if you're worried, there'll be a cop here shortly."

"I'm okay." She pulled away and went back to her cleaning. "How long are you going to be underfoot here?"

"About five seconds."

"Didn't you tell them you'd wait for your bodyguard?"

"As a matter of fact, I didn't."

"So what are you going to do in five seconds?"

"Ask you where I can find Mr. Smith when he's not in a meeting."

25

Jody said that very few FREE members knew where Smith lived, and they kept it secret. Otherwise, a man like that would never get any peace. He might be at the Village headquarters.

He wasn't. And no one at the headquarters would give his address. Thinking there might be someone on the street who was a weaker link in the FREE organization, Steve asked if there were any campaigns going on that day. Yes, the Bronx, Harlem and the Bowery.

The Bowery was closest, so he went there. If there was a campaign going on, he saw no evidence of it. There was a need for help, though. Here there were more bums and winos per square foot, he thought, than in any other part of the city. Within a two-block walk, Steve was approached seven times. In another part of town, he might have parted with a quarter or two. But a single act of charity here would attract denizens the way a garbage truck attracts flies. And Steve didn't want to attract attention.

He thought things were looking up when he found a working telephone. Three others were out of order.

"Any messages for Steve Hershey?"

"Oh, my god, yes. Now you stay right there, will you?"

"Definitely."

A moment later. "Moe-somebody has called you four times today. He doesn't leave a number but keeps saying he'll call back."

The other messages were from other clients who were beginning to feel ignored. While Steve had nothing else to do, and a working phone to boot, he returned the calls. Moe, of course, couldn't be contacted. Steve had run out of quarters, anyway. Also, at that point, he saw a familiar face on the street.

A half block away, Sue, the girl who'd conquered her drug addiction at the FREE meeting, was walking in his direction, smiling and distributing incense packets from her knit shoulder bag to anybody who'd accept the offering. She wasn't getting many takers. The last thing anyone around here wanted was incense. One or two diehards tried for monetary contributions but gave up easily. Obviously, the girl was familiar in the area and, if there were any potential converts, they had long since seen the light or backslid with renewed commitment to their old ways.

A few doors from where Steve stood partially hidden by the phone, a hand reached from a doorway. Sue took something from the hand and put it in her shoulder bag, then brought out a packet which she gave to the hand.

She continued along her route, taking a packet from the bag and holding it ready for the next offering. Steve stepped from behind the phone when she got to it. "Pardon me."

Her smile faded. After all, he was reasonably well dressed, hadn't had a drink recently and didn't look like he needed one.

Steve saw the tired, drawn lines of the addict still etched on her face. As she recovered her smile, she held out the packet to him, and he saw the track marks of the mainliner that retreated into hiding beneath the three-quarter length sleeve of her linen blouse. On top of that, she had a cold.

"Burn this," she said, "and burn away your troubles."

"What is it?"

"Incense. FREE incense. There's a message on the wrapper. If you read it and take it into your heart, it may help you."

"Help me what?"

"Help you improve your life. Just read the wrapper."

"I have a friend who needs that kind of help. He's a gambler. Loses all his money on the horses. His wife and kids are hungry most of the time. I try to help, but I'm only one guy. Have you got something for him, too?"

She brought another packet from her bag. Steve took it. "How about the wife and kids? He's got four kids."

She was uncertain. "Show them what it says on the wrapper. It tells about meetings we have on Thursdays. Bring them to a meeting, and maybe we can help them."

"Oh, this guy doesn't go to meetings unless they're at OTB, you know? But maybe his wife could get him to come. Or the kids. Can't you spare five more?"

"I'm sorry. I'm running low, and there are so many others in need around here."

"Well, nobody's more in need than my friend and his family."

"Be here tomorrow, or come to the meeting." She walked on.

"Miss, I don't think you understand the seriousness of the situation. Miss! *Sue!*"

The sound of her name made her turn, and then she saw he had the gun pointed at her. "It's a very, very serious situation," he told her.

Her instinct for self-preservation hadn't been totally dulled, only enough to freeze her in place and keep her waiting for instructions, letting her nose run unchecked.

"Step into the doorway," he said.

When they were both in the doorway, she said, "You can have more if you want. I didn't know it was that important to you."

"Give me your bag."

"No! Please! What do you want? Money? I'll give you money." She reached into the bag and brought out a tangle of bills, maybe a couple hundred dollars. If she could get that much from a random swipe into her grabbag, there must be a lot more where that came from.

"The bag. Take it off and hand it to me."

She couldn't move. Steve reached to her shoulder and lifted the bag over her head. "Now sit down," he commanded, and she sank into a corner of the doorway.

The bag was divided into two sections. One section had incense packets with blue borders like the two she had given him. The other had packets with red borders and a medley of bills.

He unwrapped a red-bordered packet and removed the incense, then used the butt of his gun to tap off the top. Inside was a cellophane wrapper around white powder. He took it out and ripped it open with his teeth. That was enough. Even through the milk sugar he could taste the bitterness of the maybe four percent that was heroin.

26

The package contained about a quarter teaspoon of the mixture and was known on the streets as a "deck" or a "bag." Based on current prices, what was left in the bag was worth at least three hundred dollars and the cash received so far was another three hundred.

Not a big deal? If there were twenty agents like Sue, each expecting to take in six hundred a day (probably a conservative estimate), that translated into twelve thousand a day, seventy-two thousand a week (with a day off), almost three hundred thousand a month, and roughly three and a half million a year. Not bad for incense peddlers. Steve no longer wondered how FREE paid for postage.

"Take me to your leader," he said.

She tried to shrink into her corner of the doorway. "No, I can't. There isn't any leader."

"Well then, let's go see Mr. Smith." He waited with the gun pointed until she sighed deeply and nodded.

Her bag slung back over her shoulder, she started walking west toward the Village. Steve stayed about thirty feet behind her, looking casual, Bertha back in the holster.

It turned out to be a very long walk. In fact, it was about twenty-five blocks, all the way back to London Terrace, the entrance to the east Tower on the corner of Twenty-third and Ninth, the other location where the cleaning woman had worked.

Steve took Sue's arm as she turned into the lobby. The doorman recognized her and, seeing that Steve was with her, didn't question him.

They rode the elevator to the sixteenth floor where she led him to a door at one end of the hallway. A sign on the door requested visitors to remove their shoes, and there were two pair on the doormat, white loafers and brown mocassins.

"Ring the bell," he told her.

She wiped her nose with a wornout tissue.

He stood at the side of the doorway. "Go on. Ring it."

"Then what?"

"Then when somebody answers, go on in. Don't worry, I'll be right behind you."

"That's what I *am* worried about." She kicked off her shoes and rang the bell which sounded like Oriental chimes. There was no answer. Her voice had a touch of hope. "He's not home."

"Then a couple guys are wandering around barefoot." Steve reached in front of her and knocked. He had to knock a second time before it opened.

Standing there was Brian, Smith's successor. He looked like he didn't see Steve and Sue but was looking at a ghost on an imaginary screen near his eyes, like he was doped up on something. Steve pointed Bertha at Brian. "May we come in?"

Brian stepped back numbly. Steve gestured

for Sue to go in ahead of him. Once in the inside hallway, Steve closed the door and herded the couple to the living room.

After seeing Harry Maloney's dark, cluttered environment at the opposite corner of this building, Steve wasn't prepared for Smith's apartment. The walls were white and undecorated, shining brilliantly in the sunlight that filled the room. The rug was white and wooly and rose to a boxlike structure in the center of the room. The effect was blinding.

As his eyes adjusted to the glare, Steve gestured with his gun. "I'd like both of you to go sit on that window seat."

Brian didn't hear him. Sue took Brian's arm and led him to the window.

"Where's Smith?" Steve asked.

Sue nudged Brian. He looked at her. "What?"

Sue pointed to Steve.

"Where's Smith?" Steve asked again.

"Oh." Brian pointed to the box.

It looked like a giant sandbox, except you had to climb three steps to get into it, and it was filled with white foam-rubber balls about a foot in diameter, hundreds of them. You could jump in that box and bounce around for a long time without much effort.

Smith was in the box. Not bouncing. Not moving. Dead.

Steve found his voice. "Shit!" he said.

27

The hypodermic needle was still in his left arm. (Most junkies made do with a safety pin and an eye dropper; hypodermics were sophisticated and harder to hide.) There were no track marks on his arm to show he'd ever made a habit of it. Without any tolerance for the stuff, and probably using it pure, a lethal overdose was likely.

Brian looked too frail to have anything to do with this. Smith's death has been as much of a surprise to Brian as it probably had been to Smith, which would explain the semi-hypnotic condition Brian was having a hard time shaking.

Steve descended the steps and faced the two on the window seat. "Okay," he told Brian. "What about this?"

Brian started to snap out of it. "Are you the police?"

"I'm giving you a chance to rehearse your story before they get here."

Brian held his head in his hands and scrunched

up his mouth, making it hard to understand him. "I got here about ten minutes before you did, and I found him like that."

"Who let you in?"

"I've got my own key."

"Then you probably know the apartment pretty well."

"What do you mean?"

"You come here sometimes when Smith isn't here, and you pass the time looking around. It's human nature."

"I've only been in this room and the kitchen. The rest of it's none of my business."

"Did anyone else have access to this apartment?"

"Not that I know of. Getting the key was a special honor for me."

"And you could use it anytime you felt like it?"

"Well, no. Of course not. What kind of respect would that have shown?"

"How did you know when to come and when not to come?"

"We had a regular schedule."

"Then why did you need a key?"

"Sometimes he said he might be late and I should come in and browse through his library." He gestured to a white bookcase that held books with plain white dust jackets.

"You got here, and there was no answer, so you let yourself in."

"Yes."

"What about his shoes outside the door? Shouldn't they have given you a clue he was in here?"

"All I knew was there wasn't any answer, so I let myself in."

"What did you touch besides the doorknob?"

"I don't know. Nothing, I guess. No, nothing.

I'd just come in and found him, and I was still trying to deal with that when you knocked."

"Did you go into the playpen to be sure he was dead?"

"No."

"Why not? Maybe he wasn't when you got here."

"He is, isn't he?"

"Definitely."

"That's what I thought."

"Are you an expert on dead bodies?"

"No! No, I'm not an expert on dead bodies! I just knew! You guys think you have to probe and examine everything to know what's true!" He had to stop. The release of anger brought tears, and he sobbed into his hands. "I loved that man."

"You knew him well?"

"Better than anybody."

"Did he take injections when you were with him?"

"He wouldn't. He never did. I can't believe he did now."

"You saw."

"I don't believe what I saw. Mr. Smith was a good man. He didn't drink, not even wine or beer. He didn't eat meat. He was conscientious about what he put in his body. He called it a temple."

"You never saw any narcotics in this apartment before?"

"No."

"What do you know about his relationship with Sue here?"

"What relationship?"

"That's what I asked you."

Brian looked at the girl who was hunched up on the window seat, her arms wrapped around her knees, rocking back and forth. "Sue was just one of the troops. She's been coming to meetings for a few weeks, working on her addiction problem, helping us out in the field."

"The field. You mean the Bowery?"

"That was her territory, yes."

"How many others are out there in the different fields?"

"We all do it at some time or another. There are a couple hundred of us now."

"Were you out in the field today?"

"No. I came here for training. I was supposed to take over when Mr. Smith went on to his next calling."

"Where was the call coming from?"

"I don't know. He talked about Toronto. Maybe he was going there."

"Speaking of calling, are you sure you didn't try to phone for help?"

"No. I told you. Nothing."

Steve looked at the white pushbutton phone, the receiver cord trailing around in front, the cleaning woman's trademark. Using his handkerchief, he picked up the receiver and unscrewed the earpiece, then the mouthpiece, and found no bugs.

Steve showed Brian the police sketch of the cleaning woman. "Where have you seen this woman before?"

He glanced at it, then away. "I never saw her anywhere before." He turned back suddenly. "Wait a minute." He looked at it more carefully and finally shook his head.

"How about you, Sue?"

She looked at the picture and shook her head.

Steve sighed and put the picture back in his pocket. He watched Sue rocking, then asked her, "Tell me about you and Mr. Smith."

She looked up and stopped rocking. "Like what?"

"Like what really happened at last night's FREE meeting."

"I got over my problem."

"I don't want any more lying, Sue. Lying will only get you into a lot of trouble. More than you're in already. I'm going to call the police in a minute. When I do, I want to be able to tell them you're cooperating."

"I'm sorry."

"Tell me about last night."

When she got some thoughts in order, she spoke hesitantly. "Mr. Smith asked me . . . to get well at the meeting. He said . . . it was important."

"Why was it important?"

"He said . . . we needed a success with the addicts . . . right now. That it had to be me."

"What did you say to that?"

"I said I didn't think I could do it."

"Why not?"

"Because I . . . never could before. But he said he'd show me how to do it."

"How to get rid of your addiction?"

"How to . . . make it look like I did . . . make it look real."

"You mean he coached you? He taught you how to act at the meeting?"

"Yes."

"And this acting lesson made you decide to do it?"

"Yes . . . plus I had to, anyway."

"Why?"

"Because . . . if I didn't . . . I wouldn't be able to sell it on the streets any more . . . and then I wouldn't be able to keep any for myself . . . not unless I got better at the meeting."

"She's mixed up," Brian told Steve. "Can't you see that? Mr. Smith wouldn't have anything to do with heroin."

Steve reached into Sue's shoulder bag and took out a packet. He broke open the incense and handed the contents to Brian. "I think it's time you stopped pretending to be so damned innocent."

Brian was staring in disbelief at the heroin. "What?"

"I'm tired of waltzing around with you! Other people besides Smith have been killed, and it's beginning to make me touchy. Let *me* give you your next piece of training, sonny. If a man's holding a gun, don't make him touchy."

"Screw you!"

"You're not learning very fast."

"Go ahead and shoot. I don't know anything about this, and I can't believe Mr. Smith did either. If you don't know the truth when you hear it, go ahead and shoot. I'm not going to lie to stop you."

Maybe he was too noble to be real, but he wasn't going to back down. Reconnoiter.

"Okay, I believe you. You didn't know some of your people were dealing drugs, and you don't think Smith knew about it." Steve returned the gun to its holster. "But this is the way I have to work, see. Because hoodlums love masquerading as saints. You just don't run into real saints in my line of work. So if I see someone who looks like one, I naturally figure he's a hoodlum in disguise."

"You shouldn't be so suspicious."

"I'll work on it. Now will you help me? Who knows? Maybe we can clear Smith's name."

"How can I help?"

"Tell me how the incense got to the streets."

"Most of it gets handed out at the meetings. Members can pick it up at headquarters, too. I got mine when I came here."

"Who else got it here?"

"Sue did. I don't know if there was anyone else."

"Where did it come from in the first place?"

"I don't know where Mr. Smith got it."

"How many different kinds of wrappers were used?"

"I guess two, so far."

"What two?"

"We had one printed up about FURious. The regular ones had a message about our organization and the Thursday meetings."

"These wrappers had colored borders?"

"Blue."

"What about the red one?"

"What red one?"

"Do you know Jody Stewart?"

"Sure."

"Who broke into her apartment today?"

"I didn't know she was broken into. I haven't talked to her today."

"Who distributed the incense at the FREE meetings?"

"I don't know his name."

"Was it always the same guy?"

"I guess so. I don't know. I got mine here."

"Okay. Now will you just keep Sue here while I look around?"

Brain shook his head, unable to deal with all the dirty pieces that had suddenly fallen into his pure life. "Okay, whatever you say."

Steve went through every container in the white kitchen and each one held what it was supposed to.

The bedroom. More white. White clothes hung in the closet.

The bathroom. White again. Steve's reflection in the mirror looked flushed and haunted.

The place was clean.

It was also too small. The hallway was longer than the single bedroom off it. But beyond the bedroom door was only a bookcase. Steve called Brian who appeared by the living room entrance to the hallway. Steve pointed to the bookcase. "How do you open this?"

"How do you open *what*?"

"The bookcase."

"You *don't* open a bookcase."

"You do this one."

"Who are you? Charlie Chan?"

Steve found a small button on the left side of the bookcase, pushed it, and with a little pressure, the bookcase swung back revealing a door. The door was a surprise because it was brown. Steve glanced back at Brian and was pleased to see an amazed expression on the young man's face.

"Ah so!" Steve said. Then, "Go on back to Sue."

Smugness was brief. He'd done a stupid thing. Belatedly, he checked the inner edge of the bookcase for wires that might lead to an alarm system. Luckily, none. He carefully checked the edges of the door and looked for a keyhole that might be used to set an alarm system on the other side. Again, none.

The door was locked, but a skeleton key took care of that. When the door opened, a light went on automatically inside the secret room.

No whiteness here. In its drabness the room was a visual relief from everything outside it. It stank of incense. Along two walls stretched a very utilitarian work table with the dark powders labeled by scent, something labeled "solidifying agent," and molds. A single mold for incense incense and a double mold for heroin-holding incense. One cardboard box under the table held blue-bordered wrappers, and another had red borders. There was a big bin of milk sugar. But the key ingredient was missing.

If Smith would hide a door with a bookcase, he might have been inspired by the same fictions that gave Steve detective fantasies. Steve rapped his knuckles along a wall. After a rhythm of hollow sounds, alternating at regular intervals with solid sounds where the studs were, Steve rapped a different note—neither solid nor hollow but somewhere between the two. A cavity that held something. He found the hairline crack that outlined the panel and no wires. He hit the wall around it until he found the pressure point that made the panel open.

There it was. Long plastic snakes of white powder.

Steve didn't touch the evidence. He had meddled enough in police business. And in the lives of others. Ann Brewer, Harry Maloney and now Mr. Smith. Each had died after meeting Steve for the first time. His was the handshake of death, he thought.

But he spotted something hanging behind the heroin tubes. He reached inside and felt a garment hanging on a woden hanger. He fished it out and held it up to the light. It was the dress worn by the cleaning woman who had carried Ann Brewer's body to Steve's office, who had given Steve the Mickey, who couldn't be found. Hanging around the hanger's hook and partly hidden by the flowered frock was a plastic grocery bag. Inside were the cleaning lady's shoes, gloves, lipstick and hair.

He imagined the cleaning lady without these things, and the curse was broken. Someone had died whom he'd met more than once, after all. When he'd finished his mental striptease he saw Mr. Smith holding a mop pail in his left hand. He knew that the cleaning lady had not killed Smith because Smith was the cleaning lady. And he knew it was murder because a left-handed man doesn't give himself an injection in his left arm.

28

Steve sat by the front window of Scotty's bar on Ninth. He was incidentally there for coffee and principally there to watch the entrance to Smith's building.

While he waited, he checked the name he'd written in his notebook, the one that had been listed for Smith's apartment on the lobby directory. "S. Thursh."

A squad car sirened its way across Ninth Avenue and pulled up. Two uniformed men rushed into the building. Crawford and Tonto drove up a few minutes later. They screeched to a stop and were almost hit in the rear by a guy from the Medical Examiner's. Why was everyone in such a tearing hurry?

Steve got change and called Jody from the pay phone.

"Hi. You alone?"

"Yes," she said. "Finally."

"Is anyone watching your building?"

A moment later she told him, "Don't see anyone. But somewhere out there, some of New York's finest are very angry with you."

"Afraid that'll get worse before it gets better. Look, I've got to get off in case they've got a wire on your phone. Can you meet me at the watering hole?"

"You mean . . .?"

"Where we were last time?"

"I guess so. Why?"

"I think, before long, I'll be needing help from another civilian, and I ought to keep you up to date. Also, I've got some bad news, and I'd rather you heard it from me."

"What a day!" She said. "Give me half an hour. They're fixing the door right now."

Steve walked the seventeen blocks to the White Horse. When Jody got there, she found him at the same table they'd shared last time. She touched his sleeve as she sat. He looked up, troubled about making her bad day worse. He postponed the inevitable by asking about her encounter with his bodyguard candidate (not pleasant), whether or not she thought she'd been followed (no).

Steve brought his chair closer when the juke box started in the bar. "I've got some news for you, like I said, and it isn't nice. You want a drink first?"

"Silly question."

"Okay." He rubbed his face. "I'm sorry, Jody, but your Mr. Smith is dead."

"What?"

"I saw him."

"How?"

"Murdered with an overdose of heroin."

"No, I can't believe that."

"He was obviously involved with some tough

customers. He just wasn't what he seemed to be. I don't suppose you'll want to believe he was putting heroin on the streets, either, will you?"

She shook her head.

"Jody, I saw the operation in his apartment." He let her have all the time she needed to absorb the news. When she began to crumple, he put his arm around her. "I know how it must hurt."

"What difference does it make now? It was all a lie, wasn't it?" She shook her head in disbelief. "What's good to drink?" she asked.

"These days ladies order white wine."

"I'll have a double."

"They don't come that way." He motioned to the waitress and ordered the wine and an ale.

Neither of them said anything until the drinks came. Jody sipped her wine, closed her eyes for a while, then sipped again.

"I feel betrayed," she said. "Really deeply betrayed."

"I'm not surprised. You *were* betrayed, along with a couple hundred others. You were just part of the diversion from what was really going on."

"It all sounds so improbable to me."

"I guess that's what made it work. You told me Smith took chances. He took a lot more than anyone dreamed. And they paid off. Who'd think anyone was going to such elaborate lengths to deal drugs? Starting FREE, establishing a reputation for good deeds, then under the cover of that . . ."

"We were outside Maloney's apartment building when he died."

"You were a diversion from that. Can you remember? Was anyone special in charge?"

"No. The chanting got louder a few times, but it always started way up ahead in the line."

"Well, it was probably one of Smith's partners in crime."

"How many partners were there?"

"Oh, I think most were innocent, like you."

"Was Brian in on it?"

"Not very likely. So he'll take over, and FREE will become what it was supposed to be all along."

She shook her head. "I don't see how I can have anything more to do with it."

"Don't throw out the baby with the bath, Jody."

"What?"

"Never mind there was deception in FREE. Where would the city be if everyone in it got obsessed with a single negative experience? Personally, I'd hate to see FREE go under because of this. Sure, there was a lot of crap going on, and a lot of you were being exploited. But what FREE pretended to be was still good, and you guys did some nice things for this city."

She looked at him for a moment. "Do I know you?"

He put on an expression of exaggerated sincerity, the way some of his classmates did in college when they were about to say what he was about to say. "Does anyone ever *really* know another person?"

She giggled, and they both felt a little better. She finished her wine. "That was good."

He ordered two more drinks.

"Steve, my place was ripped off to get the incense, right?"

"Remember when you took an extra package at the last meeting? You got one you weren't supposed to have, one with heroin inside it. And they had to get it back before somebody tried to light it."

"Do you know who did it?"

"The guy who was handing out incense at the meeting, he knew what was going on. It could've been him. The cops'll be rounding up these guys now. They'll probably get most of them."

"Only most?"

"Organized crime's got to be involved for the operation to have survived this long. And that means the thing's set up so that each guy only knows his part of it."

"Mr. Smith was Mafia, Steve?"

"Not really. Auxiliary status at most. I figure he had to be the one who murdered Ann Brewer and carried her body to my office. Professionals don't pull grandstand stunts like that."

"Not even as a warning?"

"They don't fool around with warnings very much. But it fits Smith. One of his roles was the cleaning lady, so that should give you an idea what kind of comedian he really was."

"This is too much."

"Oh, he was the cleaning lady, all right. The way they both loved to play with words, for instance."

"Like 'FREE'?"

"And the cleaning lady saying she belonged to something called CLUE. The guy puts on an outrageous disguise and that's all I see. I fell for it just like everyone else."

She ran her fingers slowly around the rim of her glass. "No, not like everyone else."

"Huh?"

She looked up at him. "Not like everyone else. You fell for it in your own special way."

He thought she was flattering him. "I got a special way?"

"Sometimes you're very perceptive about people. You always have been with me."

"Yeah?"

"Then there's the other side of you, the part that accepts some people at face value."

"Like the cleaning lady."

"Yes... and your detective friend Crawford, too. Who did you say he reminded you of?"

"James Gleason."

"Yes. And he's getting more crotchety all the time, just like the characters Gleason played."

"He is!"

"Sure, but I see more than that. I see an old cop who's irritable because he's about to retire and he doesn't want to. I mean, you take some people, label them as stereotypes and let it go at that."

"Well, maybe."

"Same with the way you label people New Yorkers, out-of-towners and waffles.

For a minute, he still thought she was flattering him. Then he wondered if it only sounded like flattery because it came from someone who was in love with him. She never said she was. But it was a nice thing to wonder about.

29

Saturday, April 28

Saturday night is the loneliest night in the week, according to the old song, circa World War II. It still seemed true.

On another Saturday night, Steve would be with Jody. He'd gotten used to that, started looking forward to it, and it helped get him through some tough weeks. Tonight represented a two week break in the routine. Last Saturday he'd been on Ann Brewer's trail. He wasn't with Jody tonight because, with her, he could be too easily found by patrolmen, detectives, Mafia members, auxiliary Mafia members, persons yet unknown, and now the Narcotics Squad and maybe the FBI. He couldn't return to his own place for the same reason. Hence, his second night in a cheap hotel room and the depression that went with it.

He had two consolations. One was a vigilante temper that could be aggravated into overriding other feelings. The other was the Jack Daniels, a reward for his enforced monasticism and a flamboyant gesture to a transient life. If he ever got out of this alive, he would never bother drinking cheaper stuff again.

For half an hour, he'd been doodling on hotel stationery and fantasizing like a schoolboy about being a paperback private eye holed up in a hotel room with bourbon. Steve Hershey—rough, glamorous tough guy. A neon sign was flashing through his window. In a minute, he'd probably start hearing a saxophone.

Jody had hit it on the button. He did lean toward stereotypes. But some people *were* cartoons, weren't they?

It was too early to go to bed, and he was getting bored with doodling. He'd already tried the Gideon Bible but lost interest when he got to the begat chapter. He never could bring himself to skip over that stumbling block, and with his attitude he'd never find out how the book ended.

Maybe if he charted the begats. He started with a diagram showing who begat whom, and it got to be a little more interesting until his mind wandered somewhere between Adam and Noah and he started imagining other names. Moe and Gloria and Harry Maloney begat Steve's involvement and the death of Ann Brewer . . . begat his deeper involvement . . . begat the death of Maloney . . . begat Steve's involvement with FREE . . . begat Jody's taking the wrong incense . . . begat his finding Smith's body . . . begat his uncovering of the heroin distribution network . . . all of which begat JD and the cheap hotel room.

He took another piece of stationery and started over. This time he charted the case itself, starting at the bottom with the things he was sure about, then putting blanks at the top.

SHIPMENT

_____ *to* _____

Disguise: _____

Diversion: _____

RECEIPT

_____ *to* _____

Disguise: _____

Diversion: FURious

DISTRIBUTION

Thursh (Smith, Cleaning Wm.)
to
Bad Street FREEbies & St.

Disguise: Incense

Diversion: FREE

It was like algebra. You started with what you knew, and that showed what you didn't know. Steve knew there were probably as many levels in the shipment and receipt ends as there appeared to be in the distribution. Similarly, if there was disguise and diversion in distribution, there probably was in shipment and receipt. FURious, a fad destined to pass, was an obvious diversion at the airport, like a flag being waved to make you look away from something else. And if FURious was meant to be expendable, then maybe the whole operation was supposed to be, too. That led to some other theories and some ideas about what had to be done next. And that begat more indulgence in JD and smugness.

Sunday, April 29

Crawford turned out to be even more irritable in the mornings, even over the phone from Bronxville.

"Who is it? I'm leaving for Mass."

"Steve."

A magic word that triggered a litany of opinions about Steve's ancestry, along with a few invectives Crawford would have to confess to the priest later. When he calmed down, he said, "You son-of-a-bitch, we've been looking all over for you! Where the hell are you?"

"Ask me no questions and I'll tell you no lies."

"Get your ass down to the house right away!"

"With murders this week on Monday, Wednesday and Friday, you want me to go out on a Sunday?"

"Have you ever heard the one about obstructing justice, Steve?"

"Later on, Crawford, you can have your way with me. Right now, you'd better let me call some of the shots."

"Why the hell should I?"

"It's your only choice. Now what have you found out since our last chat?"

"That you're a son-of-a-bitch."

"What else?"

After Crawford managed to switch channels, he said "Well, guess what? That Mr. Smith was the cleaning lady."

"Yeah, I knew that."

"When we showed his picture to the man in your building, he recognized it. Smith had been there twice, once carrying what might've been a laundry sack."

"That's how the so-called lady got in and out without being seen."

"As a man named Smith, yeah. Second time he was there he must've changed into the cleaning lady disguise after he got to your floor. There's more about that character. From Smith's fingerprints, we were able to trace him to the same Army outfit Jonathan Maloney was in."

"Figures."

'It gets more interesting. There was a smuggling operation in that outfit when they were in Vietnam together. Somebody was smuggling junk to the States in the coffins, and even the bodies, of guys killed in action. Smith and Maloney were both on the record because they'd been known to do the thing with marijuana, so they were both investigated. But the Army's CID unit couldn't connect them to the smuggling. By the way, the guy's name isn't Smith. It's Thursh. Simon Thursh."

"Figures."

"How does it figure?"

"He liked playing with words. Simon Thursh . . . Mr. Smith."

"Steve, you're sounding omniscient today. You know that? And you happen to be teeing me off."

"What did I say?"

"You keep saying things frigging *figure*. If you've got everything figured out already, why don't I just shut up and listen to you? Maybe I could be the one who gets to say he told you so."

"Okay. Sorry."

"Give you another chance. This Smith who is Simon Thursh is the same guy the cleaning lady was working for. Thursh came to the station house and described his own damned disguise for our artist. How's that for chutzpah?"

"I'll be damned!" Steve said and gave Crawford a few seconds to enjoy his triumph. "Can we get the names of any others who were investigated at the same time on that Army thing?"

"Feds are working on that. Maybe Tuesday."

"I don't think we've got that much time."

"We got to stand in line at the computer, Steve. Maybe the President could hurry things up. Why don't you give him a call?"

"Crawford, don't you get the idea that things are being neated up?"

"What?"

"Harry Maloney dies from his own booze. Smith/Thursh from his own dope. Deaths like that must've been planned a long time ago."

"Could be."

"Thursh's death kills the distribution."

"It figures," Crawford said.

"So maybe something similar's in store for the shipping end. It may be dying even as we speak. Where's the stuff going to go now?"

"Hell, we're following up on all the leads we've got. What more can we do?"

"Could you skip Mass today? Maybe take in a doubleheader next week?"

"What the hell for?"

"Because I think I can help you today if you can help me."

"I'm waiting."

"Get Jonathan Maloney in for some more questioning."

"That's pretty much up to the narcs now."

"We've still got a handful of murders to worry about. Can't you question Jonathan about Thursh? Think about your clearance rate."

There was a silence at the other end. Crawford said, "Say I help you like you're asking me to. What am I helping you do?"

"If I told you, you'd have to tell me not to. It's something you'd rather not know about."

"I sure as hell do want to know!"

"Have I let you down yet?"

"What do you call going into hiding?"

"How long have we known each other, Crawford?"

"These days, I'm not counting."

"A long time. Now, you know as well as I do that I can do things you can't because you got rules you can't break. You put a bodyguard on me and I've got to play the same game. But you keep me solo and I can break your rules. See? I can do the things you'd like to but can't. And if I split on my own and don't cooperate, you haven't got anymore responsibility to protect me."

"I don't know if Vitale'll see it that way."

"If it comes to that, I'll convince him what an unreliable guy I am."

"Suppose you get killed first?"

"Give me a break, Crawford. You think you can get Maloney to the house about one?"

"How can I let you know?"

"I'll know. Aim for one. And keep him there until you hear from me. Also, see if you can line up a judge for a search warrant."

"Off the record, Steve, what are you going to do?"

"Forget what I said about staying inside today. It's Sunday, right? I'm going visiting."

30

Half past noon. A black limo pulled up next to the awning of the expensive apartment building on upper Park Avenue. The chauffeur got out and went inside. A moment later, he returned, stood on the sidewalk and lit a cigar. He wore a sharkskin suit that couldn't hang fashionably on his chesty build.

Steve was on the other side of the street, sitting at the wheel of a taxicab with the off-duty sign lit. He wore dark glasses, munched on a tuna-fish sandwich and pretended to read the sports section of the Sunday *Times*. The rest of the paper was in the back seat. So was the real cab driver, doing the crossword puzzle, sprawled out so he couldn't be seen from outside.

"What's a three letter word for Hawaiian wreath?"

"Lei."

"Come on!"

Steve spelled it. "L-E-I."

"Oh. You done with the sports section yet?"

"Don't talk so much."

"Nobody can see me."

"They can see me answering you."

Steve glanced at the man across the street. Remembering Jody's comment about his penchant for stereotypes, Steve wondered if he should consider the psychological depths of this man. No, to hell with it. The guy was a goon.

The goon littered the street with his match, took a couple puffs on the cigar, looked up and down the Avenue, then got back into the limo and waited.

"My name's Fred," the cab driver said. "Fred Eisenberg."

Steve took a bite of his sandwich. "Saw that on your card."

"My friends call me Freddy. Maybe you should, too."

"You figure me for a friend now, Freddy?"

"Well, you did call, right? It isn't like it was a one night stand. Though it was a hell of a night and I thought you were mad at me, you did call."

"Let me ask you a personal question, Freddy."

"Those are the best kind."

"Are you gay?"

"Isn't everyone?"

"No."

"You're not?"

"No. You understand we got strictly a business deal here," Steve said. "I called you because we already got time invested, and I didn't want to have to break in a new driver."

"Okay."

"I mean we're a little bit used to each other now."

"Okay to know your name then?"

"Steve Hershey. I'm a private investigator."

"Terrific. Macho. We looking for more furs?"
"Maybe."
"Terrific. Steve . . . they call you Stevie?"
"No."
"Can I?"
"No."

Jonathan Maloney came out of the apartment building, said something to the driver, then let himself in the back seat. The car moved downtown.

"Stay low, Freddy."

Steve got out of the cab and walked half a block to a phone booth. He dialed Jonathan's home number, let it ring several times, then hung up. He tried again to be sure he hadn't gotten a wrong number. The ring sounded the same, and there was still no answer.

Back at the cab. "Okay, Freddy, time to get in front."

Freddy took the dark glasses, put them on and climbed over to the front seat. He slouched to approximate Steve's height.

'Nice touch," Steve said. "Enjoy the sports section."

"You done with your sandwich?"

"Help yourself."

"Any last instructions?"

"Yeah, be here when I come out, and be ready to move."

"Roger."

The door to the service entrance was locked. Steve opened it in the customary way. Because it was Sunday, the janitor wasn't in the cellar. But the boarded-up dumbwaiter was.

The boards pulled away like balsa wood. The inside of the dumbwaiter smelled like a forgotten crypt. Steve climbed in. Another six inches taller and he couldn't have made it, but the compactness of his build was perfect for this kind of conveyance.

And, luckily, claustrophobia wasn't one of his problems.

Unluckily, acrophobia was.

As he pulled on the rope and lifted himself up the shaft, he tried to keep his thoughts on counting the floors as they passed by.

One . . . two . . . three . . .

He tried not to think that it wasn't necessary, that the only real significance of each floor was it was higher than the one before.

Four . . . five . . .

Actually, when he reached the top, he'd be at his destination. The penthouse is always the top floor.

Six . . .

Hey, isn't this better than trying to get by a doorman?

Seven . . . eight . . .

Lay them straight. Oh shit! Pick up sticks. The image of Steve and the broken wood of the dumbwaiter lying at the bottom of the . . . sh-a-a-a-ft . . .

NINE . . . NINE . . . NINE . . . AND-A-TEN . . . TEN . . . TEN . . .

He was sweating now. Partly the exertion of pulling himself through this airless space . . . sp-a-a-a-ce . . . Think of a nice hot shower . . .

Eleven . . . eleven . . .

On my way to Heaven. Another old song. Yeah, a shower . . . and some JD.

Twelve . . . thirteen . . . no, fourteen . . .

When the faint cracks of light from unused dumbwaiter doors became blurry, Steve wiped the sweat from his eyes.

Fourteen . . . no, *fifteen* . . . sixteen . . .

So many unused dumbwaiter doors. A wonder the cracks hadn't sealed up with dust over the years. Over the years. How many years? How long had these ropes been rotting in this sh-a-a-a-ft?

SEVENTEEN ... seventeen-seventeen-seventeen ... EIGHTEEN ... eighteen-eighteen-eighteen ...

Think of it this way. It's a short way *up!*
Nineteen ...
Almost ...
Twenty!
Penthouse! Everybody out.

The oblong crack was brighter here. Closer to the sun? No, the light was on in the kitchen. Did someone come in during the last eternity? He heard the phone ringing in the kitchen. He waited. It rang several times before it stopped. Then silence.

That's when the ropes snapped.

31

He held his life on the palms of his hands that were braced on the small ledge of the dumbwaiter opening, supporting his own weight and that of the dumbwaiter which rested heavily on his neck and shoulders. He heard the ropes beneath him slapping against the shaft in their death throes.

Okay. He'd done lots of one-arm pushups. This was no different, except for the extra weight on his shoulders. With the slow precision of a bomb squad, he shifted all the weight to one hand and beat against the door with the other. One! Two! Three! The door caved in. His free hand went quickly back to the ledge, and as he held the weight with his palms again, he slowly uncurled his body over into the brightly-lit, ceramic-tiled kitchen, still holding the dumbwaiter up with his feet.

An awkward posture, his torso hanging over the dumbwaiter opening and over a straight-backed chair, his feet holding the dumbwaiter from falling.

He lifted the chair, turned its seat away to his left and wedged its back into the opening. Then he slowly let the dumbwaiter settle until its weight rested on the chairback.

He dove into the room, cushioning his fall with a forward somersault from the neck and rolling to his feet. He spun around at the sound of the chair cracking, reached in to hold the dumbwaiter up, pulled out the chair, turned it around and shoved it back legs first. He waited to see if it would hold, and it did. Only when he was satisfied with the success of his engineering did he begin to feel dizzy.

He sat on the black tile floor until the spinning stopped. The silence was beautiful.

Gradually, he became aware of a pain in the back of his neck where a splinter from the smashed door was embedded. He yanked some of it out. What was left inside made his neck hurt worse, and there was some blood. He got up and ripped a paper towel from the wall roller.

Holding the towel at the back of his neck, he walked through the rest of the apartment, getting the lay of the land.

Jonathan Maloney lived well.

Off the shiny, neat kitchen, the dining area was furnished with highly polished Danish pieces, a crystal chandelier centered over the table, the walls covered with antique tapestries.

The thick brown rug waterfalled over into a step-down living room area. More Danish furniture with lots of pillows. There were windows with cedar blinds on two sides. Where there weren't windows there were floor-to-ceiling mirrors or rich wood paneling. On the wood hung three nudes that were original, erotic and probably very expensive. Some tree-size plants. Fashion magazines. Doors.

The first door was locked, and Steve used a

skeleton key. Beyond the door was a bedroom with a four-poster. There was a large bath with an absence of toothbrushes and toiletries. A closet door was locked. Opening this, Steve saw it contained electronic equipment.

He flipped a switch on. Over a speaker came the sound of heavy breathing, not like a dirty phone call, more like explosive exhalations. Familiar, the way a face on the street—a waitress at a favorite restaurant, the guy who hands out towels at the Y—can't be placed out of its normal environment. Steve puzzled over the sounds a moment, then turned off the machine.

He returned to the living room and started for the second door when, Columbo-like, he snapped his fingers and returned to the bedroom closet. This time, along with the exhalations, he heard metal hitting wood—the sound of weightlifting. Big Moe's apartment had been bugged when Steve was there and unknowingly told the world that he really wasn't going to Iroquois, Illinois.

He shut off the machine and retraced his steps to the door he hadn't opened yet.

Another bedroom. An unmade waterbed. Male and female clothing scattered about. So Jonathan wasn't actually living alone at the moment.

Steve raised the cedar blinds and looked to the street below. Freddy's cab was still there. That was especially important now. Since Steve couldn't get out the same way he got in, the doorman would see him and a quick getaway might be necessary.

But he hoped to find something more damning than the bugging equipment to justify a search warrant—especially one on a Sunday, the hardest kind to get—to bring the police, to keep Jonathan at the station house, to minimize the chances Steve would have to escape through gunfire from Jonathan's goons.

Two more doors to check. Another bathroom. Another closet.

As he neared the bathroom door, he could hear a shower running. Either Jonathan was more careless than he looked or somebody else was here. Maybe somebody who took long showers and didn't hear the phone ring. Or, he looked at the panties and bra on the floor near the bed, somebody who wasn't supposed to answer the phone.

He ought to get out. But if he continued to be lucky, a shower that had been running this long wouldn't stop now.

He went to the closet. It wasn't locked. He stepped inside and turned on the light as the door swung shut behind him. There were two rows of suits and sports jackets and still plenty of room to walk around. Two rows of men's shoes displayed against the back wall. A tall tower of folded shirts. And hanging amidst the suits, a big, bulky FURious.

Just as he was taking it off the hanger, the closet door opened. He automatically reached for his gun, crouched and spun around, pointing it up to where the person's chest would be.

It was a very nice chest. It had a towel draped over half of it. And that's all Kansas Gloria was wearing.

32

Steve was just as surprised as Gloria. Besides that, he was embarrassed to be found in a closet. "Hello," he said.

She swallowed. "Hello."

"I'm not going to hurt you."

She nodded hopefully. She looked down at her body, then looked up like Eve who ate the apple and couldn't find a figleaf anywhere. Steve handed her the coat, and she put it on.

"Please don't shoot, okay?"

Steve had forgotten the gun, and he lowered it. "No, I mean it. I'm not going to hurt you." He returned Bertha to the holster and rose to all the height he had.

A flicker of recognition on her face. "Do I know you?" She changed her mind quickly. "No, no, I've never seen you before in my life."

"Try to relax, Gloria. It's okay."

"Are you sure?"

"Yes."

"You're Moe's friend, aren't you? You don't have to answer if you don't want to."

"Steve Hershey. We met at his place once."

She sat on the waterbed. Steve sat beside her. The waves were distracting. So was a naked girl in a fur coat. He suggested they move out of the bedroom. As he followed her, he watched the fur move just as Max Senior had described. It was alive, moving in response to her movements, heightening her sensuality almost to the point of comedy. Gloria sat in one of the Danish chairs. Steve felt a need to stay on his feet and pace.

"Now, Gloria, what're you doing here? Are you Jonathan Maloney's girl friend? Because that's the way it looks."

"Yes, I guess I am, in a way."

"In what way?"

"Well..." She looked toward the bedroom, Kansas Protestant in conflict with Gold Coast paramour. "Well... you know."

"How long's it been going on?"

"What's today?"

"Sunday. Sunday, the 29th."

"About five days, then, I guess. I'm not sure."

"Since Wednesday?"

"I think that was when I came."

"Have you been here ever since then?"

"Yes."

"You never went out?"

"No, I couldn't."

"Has he got you prisoner here?"

"No. He's protecting me."

"From what?"

"From whoever killed Ann."

"Who would that be?"

"Whoever. Jon's brother?"

"No. Anyway, he's dead."

"That's right. I must've blocked it out. Who

killed him?"

"A cleaning lady named Mr. Smith is my guess."

"Is he in jail?"

"No, he's dead, too."

"Who killed him?"

"We don't know."

"Then maybe I still need protection."

"Yeah," Steve had to admit, "maybe you do. But I'm not sure your lover's the best man for the job."

"You mean you think he killed the killer ... what's his name?"

"Mr. Smith alias Simon Thursh. No, I think if Jonathan killed Smith he'd be cutting off his own feet. But your boyfriend's involved with organized crime, you know."

"No, I didn't know, in a way."

"What do you mean, 'In a way'?"

"Well, I guess I suspected we were involved in something illegal. I blocked it out."

"And whatever it was, you and Ann were both in on it."

"Yes. Ann wanted to get out, though."

"Why?"

"She said she had a chance to make a nice, honest living."

"What chance?"

"A modeling job, she said."

Steve sighed and sat down. "Do you think her murder was connected to her wanting to get out?"

"That's what I thought at first. But then when Jon's brother was killed, too, I wasn't so sure."

"Is that what made you come here for protection, Harry Maloney's death?"

"No, Jon told me about that later. I was plenty nervous to begin with, and then when I saw the crowd outside Harry's building, and they looked angry when they saw me ... that was all it took."

"Then you were the girl wearing the fur in the taxi."

"Yes." She looked down at her garment. "This one."

"And you came here."

"Yes. Jon was nice to me when we shot the ads. He made a pass. I knew I'd be welcome here."

"Gloria, you'd be more than welcome in a lot of places."

"I would?" She blinked, impervious to her own beauty. "Really? I would?"

"Lots of places. For one thing, you could have gone to Moe. I don't know why you'd want to, but you could have."

"Oh, no! I was afraid of him."

"Weren't you always?"

'Not at first. You know, when I came on the bus with nowhere to live. Then I was scared of the city. But Moe was there—almost like he was waiting for me. He made me feel safe then. But now he doesn't. Jon makes me feel safe now."

"You had an apartment to go to."

"Anyone could find me there. I think I was even followed a couple of times."

More guilt. So Steve had been partly responsible for Gloria winding up with Jonathan. "Yeah, you were followed," he admitted. "That was only me."

Her eyes were wide. "But it scared me."

"I'm sorry. Where were you hiding before you came here?"

"At Ann's place. I got scared there, too. I mean when Ann didn't come home. Then somebody came into the apartment when I was there. It wasn't Ann."

"Ouch."

"What?"

"That was me, too, in Ann's apartment."

"You just let yourself in?"

"Where were you?"

"Under the bed."

"What did you think when Ann didn't come home?"

"First I thought she might be here."

"What would she be doing here?"

"Same thing I am. Jon liked Ann, too."

"How do you know that?"

"He let her keep one of the purses from the ads. He was sorry later. I don't know why."

"How'd you ever get involved in all this?"

"What?"

"Taking trips to the airport and so forth."

"Well, to start with, I was at Moe's, and he had a number written down, a telephone number, and the word 'models.' We'd been having an argument about something. At least he was yelling at me. And I asked him about the note just to change the subject. He said it was from an ad, and he thought maybe they'd want muscular guys like him. But it turned out they only wanted girls like me."

"Is that what he said? 'Girls like you'?"

"I think so. Sometimes I felt like he was trying to get rid of me. The big arguments. The jealousy. I couldn't take it anymore. But on what I made at Rothstein's I was kind of trapped into a . . . you know . . . life style."

"And you called the phone number."

"Yes, and it belonged to Jon's brother. I didn't know Jon yet, though, so I didn't know Harry was anybody's brother at the time. Harry wasn't so drunk that first time. He told me what I'd have to do."

"Which was?"

"Be part of some shooting sessions for some ads for a new fur coat. So I did that, and that's when I met Jon and he was so nice."

MURDER AFTER A FASHION

"You used a purse in these ads."

"Lots of them. Ann, too. Ann got to keep one. Or did I tell you that?"

"Who decided what purse you'd hold in each ad?"

"Jon did. He decided everything."

"What everything?"

"The way our clothes hung. The way we wore our wristwatches. We both got to keep the watches."

"Okay, what happened after the shooting sessions?"

"Then Jon's brother told us the rest of it. Certain days I was supposed to wear a fur to Kennedy. I went to Harry's place to get it, and he'd tell me what time to leave for the airport."

"Different times of the day?"

"Yes, it varied."

"Go on."

"Harry gave me a plane ticket."

"Where to?"

"Florida. Different places."

"Then what?"

"I was supposed to take a taxi to Eastern and stand in line until I got paged."

"Somebody paged Gloria Emery?"

"No, Harry gave me another name. His mind was fuzzier when he got to this part, after the ads were all shot, and he had to read me the name off the ticket. I was always Gilda somebody. Ann was . . . I forget."

"Frieda Friedman."

"That sounds like it."

Typical Smith / Thursh inventions, Steve thought. "Okay, so you're standing in line and you hear this phony name being paged. Then what?"

"Then I went to the phone and somebody told me what to do next. A nice sounding man. He had some kind of accent."

"What did he tell you to do?"

"Go to the ladies room near a particular gate . . . whatever gate such-and-such a flight was coming to. He'd tell me the flight, and I'd get the gate number from the board. So I did what he said and waited in the ladies room until someone came in wearing a coat like mine . . ."

"And you exchanged coats."

"Yes!"

"And the airline ticket?"

"That was in the pocket, so she got it."

"And she went to Florida or someplace."

"I guess so."

"And you went back to Harry Maloney's apartment with the coat this other lady'd been wearing."

"And I'd leave the coat with Harry. Sometimes I'd have a drink with him. I think he liked me. And then I'd go home."

"Except when you went somewhere else."

"Yes, Ann's. I finally figured it would never be any good between me and Moe anymore, and Ann understood. She made me be very careful not to leave any signs around the apartment that I was there in case Moe came looking for me."

"All the time you were making these trips to the airport, it never occurred to you what was going on, Gloria?"

"No." She blinked her pretty eyes. "But then, I didn't want to know."

A dumb blonde? A genuine dumb blonde? Careful.

"Can you remember what days you made trips?" Steve asked.

"Well, Wednesday I guess was the last time."

"Before that."

"No. I guess I blocked it out."

He sighed. "Well, did you keep a record of any kind?"

"Let me think." She screwed up her face.

"Okay, but while you're thinking, how about changing so I can look at the coat?"

"Huh? Oh, sure. You want me to change first or give you the coat first?"

"Change," he made himself say. "Change first."

"Okay." She smiled and went into the bedroom, returning soon in a flimsy silk thing, coat in hand, watch on wrist.

"Is that the watch you wore in the ads?"

"Yes." She held out her wrist. "It doesn't work. It needs a battery. Jon's going to get me one."

"Wasn't it working when the ads were shot?"

"It didn't have a battery."

"Ann's, too?"

"I guess so." She handed him the coat. "I'm sorry. I think I did have a calendar, but I don't remember where I put it. The day of the week wasn't important here, so I guess I blocked it out. That's the way I am with figures, too."

Steve spread the coat on his lap with the lining up. He felt the rolls of foam padding. Except this time, about every fifth roll felt different from the others. He wasn't going to rip it apart. He wanted the police to get the coat exactly as it arrived in New York. He'd let them discover the heroin inside it.

Seasoning the airport with FURious coats to camouflage one or two with contraband, it couldn't work forever. Somewhere a Customs person would eventually become famous over this. So, like the coat itself, the whole operation had to be designed to end, and its demise included murder. Gloria's life was in danger, too. And maybe Moe's.

"Gloria, did Jonathan ever promise to take care of Moe for you?"

"Do you mean hurt him?"

"Don't you think your new boyfriend is capable of hurting someone?"

She blinked. "Oh, no!"

He searched the coat pockets and found a small red datebook. "Oh," Gloria said. "That's where it was."

The dates were circled. In April, besides Wednesday the 25th, she'd made pickups on the 20th and 12th. The notation by the 20th said "Ann."

"Was this the day Ann went to the airport?"

"There was one day we both went, so that must be it."

It was the day when Steve had seen them both there. And the 25th, Wednesday, was the day the demonstrators had spotted Gloria in the cab.

"Gloria, I'm going to have to leave you now. But I've got to warn you Jonathan won't be coming back."

She looked more frightened than when she'd discovered him in the closet. "Not coming back?"

"The police'll be coming, though, and they'll take care of you. You won't be safe otherwise. Understand?"

She nodded.

"When they come, give them this coat and show them what's in the closet in the extra bedroom."

"What's in it?"

"Don't you know?"

"That bedroom's always locked."

"Not anymore."

He picked up the phone and called Crawford at the station house.

"This is getting embarrassing and sticky," Crawford crabbed. "We've run out of questions, and he's suspicious."

"You're off the hook, Crawford. Book him. Possession of narcotics. Get up here with that search warrant for his place, and you'll find more than you bargained for. There'll be a young lady here to help, name of Gloria Emery."

Crawford whistled. "So that's where she is!"

"I'm sure she's on a hit list, so take her into custody for possession, too. Don't worry, it'll stick."

"Anything else, sir?" Crawford was trying hard not to sound pleased.

"Yes, let's get together, shall we?"

"I can't tell you how much I'd enjoy that, Steve. Your place or mine?"

"Out at Kennedy. Near the Eastern counter. Tomorrow."

"Tomorrow's the 30th, remember? The number on the purse? We'll be there all day."

"Maybe I can save you some time."

"Tell me about it."

"Have the lab look at the wristwatches Ann and Gloria are wearing in the April ads. Then call my office and tell my service. I'll be in touch."

He hung up and told Gloria, "Until they get here, sit by that bedroom window. If anyone tries to get in before you see the police drive up, lower the blinds, and I'll come running."

She nodded and went obediently into the bedroom.

Steve made sure the hallway door locked when he closed it, then made a respectable exit down the elevator and through the lobby. He hurried past the doorman like he was on urgent business and, as is usually the case when you look like you know what you're doing, the doorman barely glanced at him. He wouldn't bother watching to see Steve get in the back seat of the cab across the street and duck down out of sight.

Gloria's golden tresses could be seen stationed at the window. She was blonde, all right, but dumbness wasn't the problem. It was her exaggerated loyalty to and dependence on others. Her inclination to take orders without questioning them. The very things that made her a perfect candidate for the operation.

Ann had been the problem. They had misread her, seeing only her great need, not anticipating such a person would get a better offer that would stimulate a latent streak of independence.

The police car drove up.

Steve spoke from the floor of the back seat. "Okay, Freddy. Let's go."

33

A call for Jody from a hotel room.

"Are you all right?" she asked.

"Except for a pain in my neck, yeah."

"I had an awful feeling today."

"So did I." He got a chill as he remembered the dumbwaiter episode. "But it's okay now. Listen, you remember my telling you I might be needing the help of another civilian?"

"Meaning me? Yes."

"Tomorrow's the day."

"When tomorrow?"

"I'll have to get back to you on that. Will you be home all night?"

"Oh, I don't know. I was supposed to go out with Brian. He wants to console me about what happened to Smith."

"Hey, I thought we had a relationship!"

"Well, I don't know. At least I'm telling you what I'm doing, and you don't tell me."

"I'm hiding from people."

"From me?"

"No. Damn it, will you please stay home tonight?"

"Okay. Steve?"

"Yeah?"

"I was only kidding about Brian."

"It wasn't funny."

"I'm glad. I didn't want you to go to bed with that on your mind."

"I think I love you, Jody."

She was quiet, then her voice was soft. "Are you sure?"

"Definitely sure I think so."

"I don't think you ever said it before."

"Did I have to?"

"Yes."

"You never told me either."

"Maybe I will now."

"Go ahead. I'm a lonely guy in a hotel room with only a small bottle of Tennessee comfort for company."

"It's your turn to wait," she said.

There was a message from Crawford on Steve's service, call him at home right away. Steve did. He couldn't see that Crawford was in his undershirt and held a martini on the rocks and that he was very careful not to let the ice rattle over the wire and modify the seriousness he always tried to convey. Crawford couldn't see that Steve had his shoes off and nursed a JD. But their two disembodied voices traveled between Bronxville and Manhattan and laid the groundwork for the next day's meeting of the bodies.

Steve asked, "What happened with Jonathan?"

"We made the connection between him and Thursh. He admitted they knew each other in the Army. He also said he'd heard something about narcotics shipments out of Vietnam, but they were only rumors. If he ever knew he'd been investigated by the CID, he'd conveniently forgotten."

"Any reaction to Thursh's apparent overdose?"

"He said Thursh once entertained the troops with a game of Russian roulette, so he might do anything crazy.

"Then Jonathan doesn't think Thursh was murdered."

"That surprise you?"

"What happened after you booked him?"

"He got mad and called his lawyer."

"You read his rights, of course."

"No, we beat him with rubber hoses! What do you think? Of course we read him his rights!"

"Easy, easy. Just checking."

"You can be a pain in the ass, you know that?"

"Definitely."

"Anyway, we were able to hold Maloney long enough to get to his apartment, and we found the stuff and Miss Emery."

"Where's Gloria now?"

"We've got her. She's okay. A little rattled, though. Her memory isn't much better than Harry Maloney's was. She on something?"

"She blocks things out."

"So she said."

"You still got Jonathan?"

"His lawyer had to do some more work, and we got a judge stalling about setting bail. We're going to try to hang onto him until tomorrow afternoon."

"Because you think we'll have more evidence then."

"Yeah, what about that?"

"Tell me about the wristwatches."

"The time was different on each one. Nobody

paid any attention to that fact the first time around because watches do continue to run during a shooting session. Except Gloria says they weren't running. And in the pictures the differences were hours apart."

"Right."

"One was 2:30, one 8:00 . . ."

"Just tell me about the one where Ann Brewer holds the purse with 30 on it."

"Just a minute . . ." He must have been checking a list. "It was 1:31 to be exact."

"Then I'll meet you tomorrow at JFK Eastern about 12:30. Listen, Crawford, maybe it's selfish of me, but do you think we can keep this case in the family?"

"Leave out the narcs? Not a chance."

"Well, maybe not a whole army of them, okay?"

"Steve, we're already stretching our responsibility here. I'm surprised they've let *me* stay on it this long."

"Well, do your best. See you tomorrow. Bring the coat."

"I can't bring the coat. It's evidence."

"Can you get another one like it?"

"I'll bring the coat. 12:30."

"Right, 12:30."

"An hour and a minute before the plane's supposed to arrive."

Steve smiled and hung up.

34

Monday, April 30

Steve fumbled a fresh pack of cigarettes from his jacket and opened them. He tapped the open end against his thumb to get them started. Several fell on the floor of the cab. He left them there, took one out of the pack, started to light it, saw Freddy's sign asking him not to and put it away. He checked his watch.

Jody watched him. "You know, you really waste a lot of energy."

"Huh?"

"All those unnecessary movements, those nervous mannerisms."

"I don't have any nervous mannerisms."

Freddy put in his two cents. "Yes you do, sweetheart."

"Who asked you?"

"It's a free cab."

"Since when?"

"No, really," Jody said. "If you could learn to

relax more, you'd have more energy when you needed it."

He looked at her, felt a pain or discomfort, a feeling hard to locate and impossible to describe. "I'm just beginning to have second thoughts."

She was suspicious. "About what?"

He looked at his watch again. "It's not too late to back out."

"What is this macho thing you've got about men being elected to take all the risks in life?"

"Would it be chauvinist to ask you if you're scared?"

"Sure, I am. Aren't you?"

"It's adrenalin."

"Then that's what it is for me, too."

"Freddy," Steve asked, "will you permit a regular customer to smoke?"

Freddy rolled his window down. "Be my guest, Stevie."

Two cigarettes later, they were circumnavigating the complex maze of roadways at Kennedy, arriving at the Eastern terminal at 12:35. Crawford was waiting outside, and his greeting was, "You're late."

"You remember Jody."

Crawford hid his irritation about her being there. "Hello again. Catching a plane?"

"She's helping us today," Steve said.

"How about the cab driver? Is he helping, too?" His head whipped back to Jody. "Sorry, miss, no offense."

Jody smiled. "None taken."

"It's just that your boy friend wanted this kept in the family, so I managed to keep it down to one narcotics man and got the airport police to stay out of it."

"Don't worry," she said. "I won't get in the way."

"Hey, Stevie," Freddy called as Steve was entering the terminal. "How long you gonna be?"

"Maybe a couple hours."

"They won't let me sit here that long."

"Freddy, work it out, will you?"

"Roger."

"There you are!" Tonto spotted them as they got inside. He had the coat over his arm. "What kept you?"

Crawford pointed to a nervous little man standing near the counter, studying the departures/arrivals board. "That's the narc. Hey, Al!"

Al moved restlessly toward them, his nervousness only apparent when standing still. His brown eyes darted around a lot, reminding Steve of a pigeon.

"Al Brenner," Crawford introduced him. "Steve Hershey and Jody . . . ?"

"Stewart," she said.

Al shook her hand warily. When he shook Steve's, he threw a questioning look to Crawford.

Crawford shrugged. "He's in the catbird seat."

"Oh, yes." Al turned back to Steve. "Crawford's filled me in on some of the cops-and-robbers stuff that's been going on. But this isn't a kid's game, you know."

"Yes, Al," Steve said. "I did know that."

"If you don't mind my asking . . ." Al looked at his unpolished shoes, then knelt to tie one of them. "Uh . . . what's in this for you, Hershey? You got a client interested in the case?"

"Not exactly."

"You're not being compensated for your participation?"

"If you mean money, no."

"Then why, if you don't mind me asking, don't

you just tell us anything you know and let us handle it?" Al rose, towering five inches above Steve. "Why? What's your motive?"

"Maybe revenge."

"For what?"

"For Ann Brewer."

"We're all of the opinion that Thursh murdered her, and he's dead now."

"I blame the whole operation, and that isn't dead yet."

"If we weren't proceeding so hastily, Hershey, we might just have some undercover people watch it until we had evidence to convict a lot more people in a lot more places."

"No time for that. It's winding down and we've got three murders to prove it." Steve took the coat from Tonto and held it for Jody who slipped into it.

Al looked around. "I've seen a couple coats like that one today. There's one." He pointed to a model walking around like she was in a fashion show. "If that's a diversion like Crawford says, and if the operation's winding down like you say, then why keep up the diversion?"

"Let me lay it out for you," Steve said quietly. "The magazine ads were the messages to the source about when somebody would be here to receive a shipment. The May issues are out now without ads, so it's winding down. In the ads, the purses showed the dates and the wristwatches showed flight arrival times."

"From where?" Al asked. "If it was from Europe, they'd have to go through Customs."

"They're going through Customs in other cities before they come here. Once the courier makes it through, it's smooth sailing, and she's hard to trace. She gets here, makes the drop, goes home under another name and maybe by a different route."

Al nodded. "It all fits so far."

"From here, it went to Harry Maloney's apartment where Thursh, as the cleaning lady, picked it up and took it through the basement to his own apartment. From there in incense to the streets."

"That's a lot of steps," Al said.

"That's the point. The source only knows the courier. The courier only knows the source and the receiver. The receiver only knows the courier and Harry Maloney. And so on. There's a lot of layers to insulate the coordinator until some of the people were scheduled to be eliminated. Except Ann wanted to get out of it early, so she had to be killed ahead of schedule."

"Just two more questions," Al said, "since you're being so good with the answers. First one: If Harry Maloney was providing the clean coats for his girls to wear here, why weren't there any in his apartment?"

"I figure Thursh brought a coat each time he took one away. No need to do that when the operation was winding down. No coats in Thursh's apartment for the same reason. What's the second question?"

"Why is your girlfriend wearing the coat?"

"Mr. Brenner," Jody said, "I don't like being talked about as though I weren't here."

"Sorry, Miss."

"This is what's going to happen," she said. "I'm going to go through all the motions of the receiver, and that way we'll get one of the couriers."

"What makes us think the courier's going to show up now?"

"One of Steve's gut feelings," Crawford guessed.

"No," Steve said. "It's more than that." He rubbed the pain at the back of his neck and felt a bump.

"Go on." Tonto's turn to be impatient.

Steve tried to shake off the pain. "It's because of those layers. I don't think the source has any way of knowing that the girl who's supposed to make the pickup was killed a week ago. All he knows is this is the last scheduled shipment."

Steve took Jody's purse, put his gun in it and handed it back to her. Jody stood in line where the men were able to watch her.

Crawford said, "That bug Jonathan's got out, Steve. Any idea where it is?"

"Not a clue," Steve lied.

Tonto prompted, "It's not a simple wire."

"Neither was the bug in my phone. What did Jonathan have to say about it?"

"Oh, he didn't know it was there. Said that closet was always locked."

"Interesting."

The announcement came over the loudspeaker. "Miss Frieda Friedman . . . Frieda Friedman . . . please pick up the nearest Eastern courtesy phone."

"Bingo," Steve said.

Jody left the ticket line and went to the phone. She said something, listened, looked up at the arrivals board, nodded and hung up.

As Jody walked by the men, she whispered, "Flight Number 14 from Miami, Gate Ten." She went on toward the gate.

After she got out of sight, the men went to Gate Ten.

In Steve's mind, it had been a simple matter of one woman exchanging a coat with another at first, with the men coming in to take care of the rest of it. And a policewoman might have aroused suspicion. He'd had some misgivings about Jody's safety, but it wasn't until now that the implications hit him hard and he knew why he'd put the gun in her purse.

Steve spotted a ladies room on the way to the gate, then walked past a dozen other gates to be sure he'd found the closest one. When he got back to Gate Ten, Crawford, Tonto and Al had taken up their positions. Tonto sat at the gate like he was there to meet somebody. Crawford stood reading a newspaper halfway between the gate and the ladies room. And Al was outside the ladies room, tying and untying his shoelaces. Steve remained beyond the gate where he could see the arrivals who were just beginning to stream in.

The suspect was one of the last through the gate, and her coat was the only FURious worn from Miami that day. She was the horsy looking, deeply suntanned woman Steve had seen here before. She talked with a stewardess as they proceeded down the hallway, the coat accentuating her rhythms. They moved past the restroom door. Al looked at Crawford, wondering maybe if the switch was going to happen. Then the woman stopped, said something to the stewardess, and the stewardess pointed back to the ladies room. The woman nodded, retraced her steps and went inside.

The wait was interminable for Steve, and he finally started toward the door. He was reaching for the knob when there were screams inside.

"Police!" Steve told the people outside and rushed in with Al behind him.

Inside, one woman huddled under a sink. Another screamed from one of the stalls, "What is it? What's going on?" The least of anyone's worries was that two men had rushed in. The focus of attention was Jody in a struggle with the horsy woman. She had Jody against the wall, pinioning the hand with the gun against the wall.

"Drop it, you bitch!" the woman screamed.

She screamed again when Jody kneed her in a sensitive spot. The woman doubled over.

"Now back away and turn around," Jody

ordered her, the gun leveled.

Still crouching in pain, the woman did as she was told. When she faced the two men, they could see she had lost her suntan and looked pale enough to be anemic.

35

She told her story in the presence of a police stenographer, Al, Crawford, Tonto and Steve. Al asked all the questions. Miss Prescott, as she called herself, gave all the answers.

Q Suppose you tell us all you know about the operation.

A A man named Carlo Gerasi manufactures the heroin in Genoa. He hired me and another girl. Her name is Maria Doria, also from Genoa. Gerasi gave us the coats and our instructions. We brought FURious coats with heroin and left with other coats. When we got back, Gerasi took the clean coats, replaced some of the padding with heroin and told us when our next trip would be.

Q How many trips have you made?

A Me personally? Eight so far. Three this month, counting today. Five last month.

Q But you didn't fly directly to New York.

A No, we always stopped over in another city. Like today it was Miami. We laid over a day, then caught the flight we were booked on to New York.

Q How did you know the person you were supposed to meet?

A I had her picture from a magazine advertisement.

Q Did you ever speak to your contacts?

A Not before today.

Q Who were you supposed to meet today?

A Frieda Friedman.

Q Who did you meet last time?

A Gilda Gill. They usually alternated.

Q The last time was when?

A Wednesday.

Q The 20th of April?

A If the 20th was Wednesday.

Q How about the other times before that?

A About five days earlier. I don't remember the others.

Q Would you be willing to submit to hypnosis to help you recall the dates?

A Yes, anything.

Q Is there anything further you would like to add to your statement?

A I'm sorry for what I've done, and I'll do anything I can to cooperate. Hypnosis, lie detector, anything.

Q And have you been advised of your rights by me? That you had the right to remain silent. That your answers might be used against you. That you had the right to a lawyer at any time, and if you couldn't afford one, we would appoint one for you. This was all made clear to you?

A Yes.

Q And you understand it all?

A Yes. I just want to cooperate in any way I can.

Q Are you cooperating with hopes of leniency?

A Not just that.

Q What else?

A Well, this is obviously a big operation. That whole FURious promotion and so forth must have cost a lot of money, and there must be some wealthy people behind it. I was paid a thousand dollars a trip. That's eight thousand I made in two months. I know if I'm making that much, the people behind it must be making a good deal more. And I was the one who was taking all the risks. I wouldn't mind that if I didn't get caught, but now things are different. I don't see why I should take the punishment for the big operators who are making the big money. The blame ought to be spread around more. It's only fair.

36

Tuesday, May 1
Now is the month of Maying
When merrie lads are playing,
Fa la la la-la, fa la-la-la-la . . .

The old high school choir song came back to Steve as he looked out his office window at the sunlit apartments across the way. May first. But the song wasn't right. Steve wasn't feeling very merrie. The pain in his neck had become figurative as well as literal. There was something about his completed chart that kept him from fa-la-laing. He turned back to his desk and looked again.

SHIPMENT

Carlo Gerasi *to* Prescott/Doria

Disguise: FURious

Diversion: FURious

RECEIPT

Brewer/Emery *to* Harry Maloney

Disguise: FURious

Diversion: FURious

DISTRIBUTION

Thursh (Smith, Cleaning Wm.)
to
Bad Street FREEbies & St.

Disguise: Incense

Diversion: FREE

Why couldn't he file it away when, on paper, all the spaces had been filled in, all the questions answered?

The thing was stopped at its source. Gerasi was out of business, and he wouldn't be making anymore calls to the Eastern courtesy phone.

Miss Prescott was in custody and Miss Doria soon would be.

Ann Brewer was dead and Gloria Emery was in custody.

Harry Maloney was dead.

Thursh was dead.

The street FREEbies were being rounded up. Those who got away were cut off from their supply.

But how did Jonathan link up with all of this? He was outside it in some way waging the FURious campaign, probably filtering Mafia funds to support the operation which must have had some heavy start-up costs. But the link between Jonathan and the rest was missing.

A knock on the door as it opened. Tonto. "What are you doing here?" he asked.

"This is my office."

"Just checking in with you. We got more information on that Vietnam smuggling deal."

"You know the third guy they thought was in on it?"

"Guy named Shaw," Tonto said. "Moses Shaw."

Steve slammed his fist on the chart. "Perfect!"

"Mr. Smith ... Simon Thursh ..." Tonto began.

"Moses Shaw ... Moe Marshall."

"They do have a ring to them, don't they?"

"And how about Gilda Gill, Frieda Friedman, Moe Marshall."

"Lovely alliteration, ain't it?" Tonto asked. "But it's still kind of slim if we're looking for a connection."

"Yeah," Steve said. "But let's assume there is one, like between Moe and Smith."

"Okay."

"Both men were planning to leave town. Both mentioned Canada."

"That a fact?"

"And Gloria's story makes it sound like Moe kind of pushed her into the Maloney setup. Moe gave her Harry's number, and he also gave her reasons to leave him."

"You're cooking, I think."

"Moe wanted me with him when Harry Maloney's body was found."

"An alibi?"

"And the day Thursh was murdered Moe was trying to reach me on the phone. Kept leaving messages that he'd be home all day. But on a day

MURDER AFTER A FASHION

like that, who was going to have time to check it out?"

"You think he just hired you for an alibi?"

"Could be."

"He didn't really want you to find Gloria for him?"

"Well, not so he could take her back into his loving arms, I'll bet. If Ann was supposed to die, it's hard to believe Gloria would get off scot free, and he might've gotten nervous about her disappearing."

Tonto smiled. "And the bug in Moe's apartment..."

"...Makes a connection with Jonathan of some kind." Steve hit the chart again, then looked up at Tonto. "You found out about the bug?"

"Yeah."

Steve was worried. "You didn't move on it, did you?"

"No."

"Then Crawford doesn't know."

"Your batting average has been pretty good. So I gave you the benefit of a doubt."

"Thanks, buddy."

"So why did you keep it to yourself?"

"A friend recently pointed out to me that I'm a sucker for stereotypes, Tonto. Well, let's suppose I've been living under a false assumption or two. Like Moe's really being such a typical dumb and strong type..."

"Then suppose he isn't...?"

"And suppose he's no more real than the cleaning lady..."

"...Or Mr. Smith."

"Tonto, if there's a Simon Thursh hiding behind those two phonies..."

"Couldn't there be someone hiding behind an ox named Moe Marshall?"

"So, there you have it," Steve said.

"What have I got?"

"I didn't want you to know about the bug, about that possible connection between Jonathan and Moe because, if I was wrong about Moe all along and he is the missing link in all this, I want to be the one who gets him."

"Doesn't the bug make it look more like Moe's in danger than in control?"

"That's one way of looking at it. But consider. Moe doesn't have a phone. Looks like he's cut off from the rest of the city..."

"But suppose the bug was there..."

"... Not so Jonathan could clandestinely listen, but so Moe could talk."

"He knew it was there?" Tonto asked.

"It'd explain the crazy way he acted when I was there a week ago. Suppose somebody on our side monitors that bug in Jonathan's apartment when I visit Moe. Maybe I can get him to admit something that you can tape."

"Yeah." Tonto drummed his fingers on the desk. "Yeah. But I'm coming with you."

"Terrific! That'll really make him open up, won't it?!"

"Suppose I stay outside."

"Well..."

"Let's call in Crawford, too."

"What for?"

"Call me sentimental. He's retiring next week. If this is the payoff, the least we can do is let him be in on it. Besides there're two ways out of that building, the street and the roof. So if you're going in, you better have two guys on the outside."

"Okay," Steve said. "As long as I'm the one who goes in."

37

Steve had to knock twice before he heard Moe's heavy footsteps coming from the front of the apartment, then Moe's voice on the other side of the door.

"Who's there?"

"Steve."

"What do you want, Steve?"

"You want to hear about Gloria?"

"Naw, to hell with her."

"You owe me money."

"Send me a bill."

"I need it now."

The locks unlocked and the door scraped partway open.

"How much?" Moe asked.

"Two hundred, plus sixty-five fifty expenses."

"Wait there."

Moe closed the door without locking it, and Steve heard the footsteps going to the front of the apartment. He pushed the door open, entered the kitchen, and saw Moe in the front room come up from a squat and spin to face him.

"Steve! Whyn't'cha wait like I told you?" He sounded offended.

The middle room was in more disarray than usual. Clothes had been strewn on the mattress. The closet door was open, the wire hangers empty.

In the front room was a half-filled suitcase on the floor and another open on the studio couch.

"You packing?"

Moe held a huge wad of bills that he'd just taken from the suitcase on the floor, held it like he'd forgotten it was in his hand. His eyes darted toward the nude painted on velvet. "Just getting organized a little."

"Organized in suitcases?"

"Oh, yeah, well, that's for later when I go to Canada for a couple days. Been planning it a long time. Gonna win that event, too."

"Good luck."

"Oh, I ain't leaving yet. I'll be seeing you again a lot before I go. How much did you say?"

"Two sixty-five fifty with expenses. You want a breakdown?"

"Naw, I trust you." Moe peeled off some bills. "Here's two seventy. Keep the change."

Steve took the money. Most of the bills were dirty and wrinkled.

"How about a beer?" Steve asked.

Moe put his foot on the iron bar of the weights and rolled them back and forth. "Take it with you, okay? I got things to do."

"Sure." Steve sat in the chair. As Moe went back to the kitchen, Steve raised his voice. "You know, that Harry Maloney thing still bothers me."

"Yeah?" Moe called from the refrigerator.

"Yeah. The cops think he drank himself to death, but I'm not so sure anymore."

Moe returned and handed a beer can to Steve. "He drank himself to death, Steve."

"I don't know. He was a professional drinker. Don't you think he'd have built up some resistance to the stuff? How many times you ever see a guy drink himself to death anyway?"

"Oh, I've seen it happen, believe me."

"You've got to be kidding me." Steve opened the beer and looked like he was settling down for a long chat.

Moe was impatient with him now. "Look, I tell you I've seen it. Now come on, I've got work to do."

"Go ahead, Moe. I'll stay out of the way. When did you ever see anybody drink himself to death?"

"Well . . . I saw it in the Army."

"Was he a wino or something?"

"It was bourbon."

"How much?"

"A fifth, a quart, I don't know. He chug-a-lugged the thing."

"And that killed him?"

"Keeled right over."

Steve took a swallow of beer. "Another thing bothers me."

Moe went on with his packing. "You worry too much."

"No, I really wonder, though. That story you just told me. It's just like one I heard from Jonathan Maloney."

"Jonathan?"

"Harry's brother. The guy who was taking care of your Gloria."

Moe's shoulders tightened. "Yeah?"

"Mr. Smith told a story like that, too."

"Who's he?"

"Oh, he's the one who was dealing heroin. Smith was being investigated for something like that when he was in the Army. So was Jonathan Maloney."

"Yeah?"

"Yeah. And now you tell me the same story. You sure you don't know those guys?"

"Don't think I do." Moe started lifting the weights, puffing with each lift.

"Another thing bothers me."

"Yeah?"

"Yeah, it bothers me to see you packing for a trip so early and taking all that money with you. If I didn't know better, I'd figure you weren't coming back."

Moe suddenly shouted, "What are you doing?!"

Steve wasn't doing anything but drinking his beer and playing cat-and-mouse with Big Moe. "Huh?"

"Stop it!"

"Stop what?"

Moe snatched the velvet painting from the wall, exposing the bug behind it. "Don't, Steve! Don't!"

Steve sat frozen as Moe smashed the weights against the bug. The thing cracked, and most of the pieces fell to the floor along with a lot of ancient plaster. Then Moe put the weights down and looked at Steve with a new face. He spoke with a new voice.

"You knew it was there, didn't you?"

"What?" Steve had trouble adjusting to the change in Moe. Moe's eyes had a glint of intelligence that didn't go away.

"You knew, didn't you?"

"Well, an apartment like this, there are bound to be some bugs."

"Trying to get me killed?" Moe smiled, no hard feelings showing.

"Why would I do that?"

"Maybe you figured the cops couldn't get me so you'd let the mob do it."

Steve didn't think it'd reassure Moe to tell him it was really the cops who were listening in on the now-dead bug. "No, Moe! I'm surprised you'd even think of such a thing."

"You've got a lot more surprises coming, Steve."

"I do?"

"You just fumbled your way into a whole pack of surprises. And if you're smart, you might even survive them."

"How?"

"Start by telling me what you know."

Steve could feel Bertha burning a hole in his pectoralis minor. "Okay," he said. "I know you're the kingpin."

"That's right."

"I think you planned it to be a limited operation."

"Right again."

"And maybe some of your partners disagreed with that part of it."

"Yeah, the bastards! What did *they* have to lose?" Moe perched on the weights bar close to Steve. "*They* were protected. *I* was the one who might get caught."

"You and a bunch of other people."

"Well, the others wouldn't get caught exactly. They'd just sort of disappear."

"To break the connections to you."

"Yeah. Simon and I had it all worked out."

"Don't tell me Thursh planned his own death."

"No, that was my idea. It was a surprise for him."

"I'll bet."

"It was kind of funny, I guess. I dressed in

white like he did, and I walked right by the
doorman. It was even easier coming out. Simon
trained me so well in the acting department, it was
a breeze. That was the funny part, how he taught
me how I could get to him."

"It doesn't bother you that you killed an old
buddy?" asked old buddy Steve.

"Ah, he would've done it to himself sooner or
later, that crazy way he lived, going out on a limb
all the time."

"He did like to take chances, I'm told."

"That's an understatement. Picture this. He
clobbers Brewer in Maloney's bed, right? What
does he do next? Get rid of the body? No. He takes
the coat with the heroin she brought from the
airport. Then he comes back, and he's right there in
the bedroom when you visit Harry. He's under the
bed, for godsake, when you're looking at the body.
He sees those special shoes of yours I told him
about and he thinks, ah ha, let's give this guy a
scare. So you go out to phone, and he takes the
body away *to your place*. It's crazy. Then he goes a
step further and shows his cleaning lady face to
you at your place. Is that enough? No! He has to
go right up to you and eyeball you at the FREE
meeting, like he was daring you to place him. Come
on, Steve. Stuff like that would've caught up with
him eventually."

"So he killed both Ann Brewer and Harry
Maloney?"

"Yeah. The mob knew about Brewer. They
didn't know about Harry. We had to make that one
look like suicide. After all . . . Jonathan's brother."

"Why did Harry have to die, Moe?"

"He was too central to the operation, one of
the links between FURious and FREE. And he
was turning into such a lush, we couldn't trust
him. So Simon took care of Harry before I took

care of Simon. I had to make that one look like suicide, too. Wouldn't want my dangerous partners to suspect I was ending the operation my way."

"I don't think you fooled them."

"Well," Moe shrugged, "maybe I bought a little time. We should've known better than to take help from the mob in the first place. Those guys just don't understand a limited operation, you know?"

"I've heard that."

"Oh sure, they'll buy it at first to get in on it. Then they get greedy. You know how it is."

"Definitely."

"Greed is a lousy thing, Steve. I guess we played on that, and it's our own fault. I mean, I worked out a deal they couldn't refuse. Right down to the last detail I had it figured out for them—cost of the ads, the coats, the models, everything. For just a half million investment on their part they stood to make almost thirteen million after Simon and I got our share."

"How much were you guys supposed to get?"

"Only a measly million, Steve. We'd split a million, that's all. Of course, Simon didn't know I was going to get all of that. But just the same! Just compare my million with the thirteen the Mafia would make on the leftover heroin we brought in for them!"

"Leftover?"

"Our setup for shipment and distribution was the part that was supposed to end, the incense and the furs stuff. After that, the mob got the leftover heroin to deal however they did it before, but without the hassle of getting it into the country. That was fair, wasn't it? But once they were partners, they wanted the thing to keep going in the same way, like furs and incense can go on forever."

"It might've worked longer."

"Maybe a little, but not much. Some of Simon's street people weren't professional, for one thing. No, the trick was to get out before anyone got wise. How much money does a guy need, anyway?"

"Can't say. You left a million hanging at the airport yesterday. How come your Mafia friends weren't there to get it if they were so greedy?"

Moe sounded like he was explaining something to a child. "Steve, you set up an operation to shield the principals, the principals don't get involved at the lower levels."

"Of course nobody cares that the courier takes the rap."

"You can't run a business on sentiment."

"How was I so lucky not to get killed in a business that doesn't run on sentiment?"

"That might've made your cop friends start taking things too seriously too soon. We didn't want to take that chance while we were still in the fur business."

"And the incense business."

"So we just wanted to scare you."

"Why'd you kill the sniper then?"

"I guess I didn't trust Jon. Couldn't be sure he didn't tell the gun to kill you after all. I couldn't have that."

"And we're such chums," Steve suggested.

"Hey, I do like you, buddy. But I needed you, too."

"To find Gloria's Manhattan hideout?"

"Yeah, just so I'd know."

"For the time when she was supposed to be eliminated."

"Yeah, but I needed you other ways, too. You were part of my cover, just like this cruddy apartment, no offense."

"And I was a good cover, wasn't I? Because I believed you were what you pretended to be."

"Aw, Steve!" Moe put back the act. "You ain't mad at me, are you?" He dropped it again. "God, will I be glad to get out of this place, and let my hair and eyebrows grow back and everything."

"So Simon taught you how to act your part."

"Yeah, I worked out the business end. But he came up with all the trimmings. He told me if you do things big enough, nobody'll see behind them. Guess he was right. I'm going to miss him a little bit."

"So are a whole lot of junkies in town."

"Well, listen, you can't keep everybody happy, can you?"

Steve was uneasy about Moe being so open, even without the bug. "I'm not too happy myself."

"Relax. You're going to be a rich man, see the world, if you want to."

"How's that, Moe?"

"Call me Mose. That's my name. Moses Shaw. My friends used to call me Mose for short."

"How am I going to see the world, Mose?"

"Why, you're going to come with me, old buddy. And I'm going to share the wealth with you. Hell, if I didn't like you, you wouldn't be sitting here now. But I got to get you out of the way somehow. I'd like it better if you came with me."

"Instead of the alternative."

"Right. But we can't waste time. I don't know how long it's healthy for me to stick around here. Understand?"

"Yeah."

"So is it a deal?"

Steve could say yes and maybe get away on the excuse of packing for the trip, but that would leave the arrest to Crawford and Tonto. If he wanted to be in on the finish of what he started, it meant a handshake now.

"Well, Mose, if I say 'shake,' are you going to crush my hand again?"

"That's Moe," Moses smiled, "not Mose."

"Okay then." Steve extended his hand. "Put 'er there."

Moses smiled again and took the hand, almost gently.

Steve stood, ostensibly to put some warmth into it, then suddenly stepped on Moses' foot and pulled. Caught off guard, Moses fell forward, and Steve shifted away to let the big man continue on his trip toward the floor. Steve leapt toward the couch and away from Moses, then pulled his gun and turned. He was just in time to see the weights sailing through the air, not in time to avoid them. The bar caught him in the chest, tripped him over the suitcase on the floor and sprawled him over the one on the couch. The gun went off and put a hole in the plaster over the couch. Moses was on top of Steve in an instant and wrestled the gun away.

"I take it your answer is no," Moses said, pointing Bertha at Steve's head.

Steve heard a shot. It took him a second to realize it had come from the street.

"You're trapped," Steve said. "That was the warning, and there's a man on his way up here right now.

Moses looked disappointed in Steve, then jolted up, the gun still in his hand, ran to the kitchen and out.

When Steve got to the hallway, he heard Crawford coming up the stairs. "Stay there, Crawford!"

"Shit on that!" The voice was out of breath and the steps kept coming.

"Stay there! He might come back. Tonto's on the roof."

Steve ran up to the roof. The roof door was

open, and he heard two shots fired. Coming through the door, he saw Tonto lying on the roof with his leg bledding. Tonto was forcing himself up to get a bead on Moses who was on the next roof and running east.

Steve whipped the gun out of Tonto's hand and took off over the roofs after Moses. "Stop or I'll shoot!" was as original as he could get. That pulled no weight with Moses. So Steve fired into the air. Moses ducked behind a low water tower on the roof two buildings away. Steve crouched behind the foot-high wall between his roof and the next and pointed Tonto's gun over the top. He was getting a sensation of *déjà vu*.

Moses' legs were exposed under the water tower. What's sauce for the goose, Steve thought, and fired. He saw the pants puncture on Moses' leg, and he heard him cursing.

Moses squatted down and shot through the legs of the water tower. Steve ducked, and the bullet whizzed over his head. He was getting to hate that sound.

When Steve ventured another look, Moses was hobbling away on his bum leg. It slowed him down, and Steve was able to catch up, close enough for a flying tackle. He landed hard against Moses' legs and wrapped his arms around them but, with the gun in his hand, wasn't able to hold on very well. Moses was able to wrench around and get into position for a close-range shot. Before he could do that, he stumbled, and Steve shot him in the foot. Moses yelled, jumped back and fell over the street side edge of the roof. Steve caught him by the ankles and held on.

Déjà vu again, but in reverse.

Moses dangled very still over the edge of the building, not wanting to struggle away this time.

"Drop the gun," Steve said, "or I'll drop you."

Moses made a fast decision, and Steve watched his expensive revolver fall seven stories. Goodbye, Bertha.

Then Crawford was there, and it took the two of them to pull the big man back to dubious safety.

It wasn't until Steve got to the street later that he realized he hadn't been dizzy.

38

Wednesday, May 2

"Okay, bite the bullet," Jody warned him, then poked into the back of his neck with a sterilized sewing needle. He counted his blessings. If things had gone differently yesterday, someone might be digging into him for something worse than a sliver.

"You shouldn't have let it go so long," she said. "It's infected."

"I was busy."

"That's what they're going to put on your tombstone."

"Cancel cancel," he said.

It was good being with Jody at her place again. It was comfortable as Sunday without the *New York Times*. Only the real estate section on the sofa was left over from three days ago.

"There!" she said and held out the sliver on the end of the needle for his inspection.

"That's all it was? That little thing?"

He started to get up, but she put her hand on

his shoulder. "Don't move," she said. She went to the bathroom and called back, "We'll have you on your feet in no time."

"Promise? I'd hate to miss Crawford's testimonial."

"You'll make it."

"Coming with me?"

She returned with a wad of cotton and a bottle of hydrogen peroxide. "Oh, I don't know. I think that's probably a boys' night out, don't you?"

"If you're asking if you'd have a good time, I don't know. But you might find it interesting. I'm going to make a funny speech."

"You hope."

"Well, they'll laugh anyway. And Crawford's bound to be good for a laugh or two all by himself."

"Is he making a funny speech?" She dabbed at the back of his neck with the cotton. "You should see this stuff fizz."

"Crawford won't try to be funny. But, you know, he'll bridle over all the fuss and probably seem more ornery than usual."

"Will the wives be there?"

"Definitely."

"Okay then, if you want me."

"Damned right I want you."

"Oh, by the way, my lease is up on this apartment in two months."

"No kidding?"

She didn't say anything, and then he realized what she was really telling him and why the real estate section was left lying around. The air was heavy with his thinking and her efforts not to. The pressure of the cotton seemed firmer on his neck.

There was still inside him an unreasonable desire to be an unattached and lonely private eye, even though it was pointless, even though, for all his freedom, gorgeous dames didn't throw themselves at his feet. When he thought about that, he began to squirm around the heart, and he heard himself clear his throat and knew he was going to say something.

"You wouldn't want to live in Chelsea, would you?"

"Not in that place of yours. That's your office."

"It's a professional apartment."

"It's where you work."

"There. See? It's like you've said a hundred times, we've each got our space when we need it. Do you really think we're compatible enough to spend seven days a week together? In the same rooms?"

"I don't know."

"See?"

"But how are we ever going to find out?"

"I mean," he changed the subject, "I really love this city—and Chelsea. I'm not sure you share that with me."

"I love the city sometimes."

"I love it all the time."

"How can you?" she asked. "Look what you've just been through. The Mafia, three murders, dope addicts. Are you telling me you love those things?"

"No, not those things."

"Do you love the fact that there's a criminal element here that's never going to be weeded out?"

"I want to be where there are people. And wherever you've got lots of people, you're going to have lots of dark corners. If you love something, Jody, you've got to give a part of yourself to it. You've got to be the light in those dark corners."

"I guess you're right," she said. "If you love something you've got to give to it."

"Right."

"You can't always be looking at the negative aspects."

"Definitely."

"You've got to take chances."

"Now you've got it."

"That sounds wise. Very, very wise."

"Yeah? You really understand?"

"I ought to."

"Why?"

"Because the way you are about New York, that's the way I am about you."

"Oh."

"So the point is, when you can accept what's wrong with a city and still be committed to it and love it, why can't you do it with a person?"

He heard her screw the cap back on the hydrogen peroxide bottle. He heard her waiting. Then he felt her hands resting gently on his shoulders.

"I love you, Steve."

He wondered if they'd be able to find an apartment in two months.